Topographia Hibernica

BLINDBOY BOATCLUB

TOPOGRAPHIA HIBERNICA

CORONET

First published in Great Britain in 2023 by Coronet
An imprint of Hodder & Stoughton Limited
An Hachette UK company

The authorised representative in the EEA is Hachette Ireland, 8 Castlecourt
Centre, Dublin 15, D15 XTP3, Ireland (email: info@hbgi.ie)

This paperback edition published in 2024

4

A CIP catalogue record for this title is available from the British Library

B format ISBN 9781529371659
ebook ISBN 9781529371635

Typeset in Bembo by Hewer Text UK Ltd, Edinburgh
Printed and bound in Great Britain by Clays Ltd, Elcograf S.p.A.

Hodder & Stoughton policy is to use papers that are natural, renewable
and recyclable products and made from wood grown in sustainable
forests. The logging and manufacturing processes are expected to
conform to the environmental regulations of the country of origin.

The authorised representative in the EEA is Hachette Ireland, 8 Castlecourt
Centre, Castleknock Road, Castleknock, Dublin 15, D15 YF6A, Ireland

Hodder & Stoughton Limited
Carmelite House
50 Victoria Embankment
London EC4Y 0DZ

www.hodder.co.uk

Dedicated to the perpetual succour of Jeff the Goblin and the bloom of uncertainty

'We are consistently losing our hedgerows, likened by one speaker to the blood supply system of the countryside. Only 2% of the country has native woodland. Over a quarter of Ireland's regularly occurring bird species are in danger of extinction. At least one third of protected species are declining in population, an invisible tragedy happening both on land and under water. Almost 30% of our seminatural grasslands have been lost in the last decade. Less than half of our marine environment can be described as healthy. Over 70% of our peatlands are in bad status and only a small fragment remain intact. The majority of our agricultural soil is in a suboptimal state, contaminated by nitrates and phosphates. Most worryingly, our water quality – the very foundation of life – is continuing to decline, with almost 50% of freshwater systems in Ireland in poor and deteriorating condition. The Assembly was told that we are at a critical juncture. Without action, we will no longer be able to rely on nature for the very services we need to live.'

– Dr Aoibhinn Ní Shúilleabháin,
Final Report of the Citizens' Assembly on
Biodiversity Loss, March 2023

'The Irish are a rude people, subsisting on the produce of their cattle only, and living themselves like animals. In the common course of things, mankind progresses from the forest to the field, from the field to the town, and to the social condition of citizens, but this nation holds agricultural labour in contempt, ignores the wealth of towns, as well as being exceedingly averse to civil institutions. Their pastures are short of herbage; cultivation is very rare, and there is scarcely any land sown. This want of tilled fields arises from the neglect of those who should cultivate them; for there are large tracts which are naturally fertile and productive. The whole habits of the people are contrary to agricultural pursuits, so that the rich glebe is barren for want of husbandmen, the fields demanding labour which is not forthcoming. This people inhabit a country so remote from the rest of the world, lying at its furthest extremity, they are thus secluded from civilized nations, they learn nothing, and practice nothing but the barbarism in which they are born and bred, and which sticks to them like a second nature.'

— Giraldus de Barri, *Topographia Hibernica*,
c. 1186 CE

Contents

The Donkey

The Donkey

There's a donkey selling Christmas trees off the round-about. Looking like a prick in the frost with a green elf's hat on its head. On journeys to visit my father I'd find myself stuck in the five o'clock traffic, forced to witness the bleedings. I'd wipe condensation from the window, and see the red tears of blood drooling down the donkey's face. And the boy in the baggy hi-vis jacket swiping in the night. The long stiff wire of a coat hanger in his hand.

Every time he hit the donkey, he'd look up to the traffic. And I'd see a confused fear wash over him. Then he'd grit his teeth and hit the donkey again. As if bateing it was something he had no control over. The jacket falling off his shoulders. His fluorescent arm pinging hot like a green laser into the side of my eye. Impossible to ignore. The cruelty of it. *Heehaw heeehaaaaaw.* Godhelpus.

And I'd see a new car parked, with red hazards

blinking. Cheerful husbands buying Christmas trees from the boy, loading them into hatchbacks, without a fuck given towards the donkey. Cunts with no hearts.

And my father's head was rotting above in St Camillus nursing home. Full of dirty knots that threw terrors at him. This made it all the worse. He was gradually being replaced by a new man, a man I'd never met, who had never met me. I put him there last June. I was eaten from the guilt of doing that. But I still endured the traffic and the abuse once a week to visit him. I'd make sure the nurses had attended to his dignity, changed his pyjamas, washed his body. This rude stranger melting in a bed. I did everything the way I was supposed to.

And then on the drives home I'd have a decent fucking cry. Fierce dramatic. The ones that start in the belly and boil hot on the forehead. I'd even go for the guttural roars. In private car darkness, no heat on so the windows fog and Ronan Keating full blast on the radio. I'd howl in a way I hadn't done since I was three. I'd blubber that he was gone but still there. I'd call him Daddy to the windshield and bawl for the shock of what he'd have just said to me.

At this hour of the rot, my father could look through

me with a polite formality, pursing his lips, as if I was serving him at a till. Or he might be a wordless newborn looking to suckle at my tit. Or other times, he'd grit his teeth with the venom you'd have for a robber in your home, and he'd reach for a mug at his bedside to assault me with. Terrified and vicious. And I didn't have words or pictures for the weight of the feelings I'd get from that. These were new feelings that hadn't been invented yet.

But the tears and the shouts stood to me in those first few months. My fists choking the steering wheel. The cries I'd have in that car would make some sense of the chaos in my belly. And that would be the end of it then for another week. When I shut that car door, that was it, out of me. Up the driveway, into the house, and off to bed. Waking up, eating breakfasts, videos of best goal compilations, cuddles with Maeve, even a few laughs with the lads in the office. I could clear through a two-foot pile of photocopying without any intrusive images of him clawing the sheets.

Until the donkey got involved. *Heehaww heehaw.* And the tears became effort – it was like trying to piss with someone watching.

Who was I to feel sorry for myself when a donkey's getting battered off a roundabout? So this one evening, I wondered to myself if my father would even notice if I was late. Would it be a better use of our time to try and intervene with the poor donkey instead? Maybe the story of it might stir something in him?

I reversed my Punto up on to the kerb and put my hazards on. I behaved like a man who was buying a Christmas tree. The boy in the hi-vis jacket was studying me the way an adult would. He was eleven or twelve with the look of parents who drank.

To his left was the poor fucker of a donkey. It had a short rope around its neck, the cheap blue cord that's made from plastic fibres. Tied around the hair. Her throat looked like someone slashed at it once a day. My heart burst acid down into my belly as I took in the landscape of her cuts.

Wafer-thin sandwich ham, flittered pink skin. She had a head like chopped wood. Pocked around her face were wounds of different ages. Some healed and some scarred. Others new, open and wet, glistening back at the frost, winking with movement.

Up close, I could see the stupid little green hat stapled to her ear. Dangling down around her cheek, I lifted it up with my baby finger. There was a colourful smell. The yellow flesh around the staples was septic and angry. Her ear was in a most unmerciful state.

My donkey inspection was making the boy fierce uncomfortable. He turned his back to me and began sparring with the night air. Someone had trained him to box like that. Making *unce unce* noises with his mouth. Darting like a pissed-off wasp. The wire coat hanger poking up from under his hi-vis jacket.

I expected a flinch, or a jock from the donkey when I touched her ear. But she didn't seem to care. Too accustomed to humans in her space. I had suspected for weeks that the donkey was female. I could just tell. In that soft way that you can gender an animal by its eyes.

'Thirty euro, for the small trees, I'll do you two for fifty, and we'll have no bother getting it in the back of your Punto either,' the boy says to me.

'I'm here about this poor donkey,' says I. 'You've her sliced up to bits. I've seen you with that coat hanger, snaking it off her face. What need is there for that?'

The boy took on a Conor McGregor pose, with his tongue out like he'd fight me. No care that I was in my thirties.

'You know nothing about her,' he says. 'She's stone mad, she gets them cuts herself inside in her pen. Bateing her head off the walls. I've no coat hanger. Search me if you want. I'm only selling Christmas trees. The donkey is for the cars. She's an advertisement. Well looked after,' he said, pointing towards a plastic bucket of orange straw in the frozen mud.

I felt a type of justified anger at the base of my spine above my arse. The one that makes you do good things. As if something beyond drove my tongue to say words.

'I'll give you two hundred euro, in cash, now,' I said. 'If you hand that donkey over to me. I'll take her, and I'll bring her to the donkey sanctuary on the north-side. She'll have a length of grass and happiness.'

A pause and a squint from the boy, and he dug his little raw sausage fingers up into his mouth, and bit on the tips.

'Howld on a second and I ring the boss,' he said.

The boy took out one of them tiny black phones that are bought for throwing away, and disappeared into a shadow.

I moved closer to the donkey. She clopped back twice and turned orange under the street light.

I could see her entire body now. The injuries from the coat hanger were mostly on her face and neck.

There were no cuts on her torso but her fur was matted and knotted from neglect. There's an accountant in work called Froggy with a Solpadeine addiction and the donkey's tail reminded me of his posture. A sad little tail weighed down by cakey dung. The steam from her nose rose high in the ice. I met her gaze, as if I had telepathy. I was hoping for something back, her voice in my head, an understanding that I was saving her. It wasn't there – she was empty from the mistreatment.

I had reached the point of no return. It was 5.25 p.m. on my watch. The Christmas traffic was very bad. If I was to opt out now, I'd never get up to my father anyway. I felt a strain of relief.

The boy returned from the far side of the round-about. The McGregor facade had lifted and he displayed the enthusiasm of a child his age, like someone had just called him a good son.

'Boss says you can take her for four hundred euro.' Chirping, with the palm of his little hand out.

I paused. Four hundred was a lot of money. I had it, but spending it on a fucking battered donkey, two weeks from Christmas? That would require a lot of explaining to Maeve, and she had been VERY understanding.

9

I slapped the boy's palm in agreement.

'Hold on and I'll go across to the ATM. Don't move from here,' I told him.

'I'm going nowhere,' he said.

The wind was blades on my face as I walked across two lanes of traffic. Cars don't really stop at that hour of the evening. People drive around you, distracted. Already have their heads on their couches with dinner and Netflix. Maybe they're all crying?

The screen of the ATM showed a balance of five hundred and eighty euro. Sure what was another four hundred with the money I'd spent on my father's care over the past two years? I withdrew the cash and returned to the boy.

Fitting an adult donkey into the back seat of a two-door Fiat Punto is difficult, to say the least. Though not impossible. I could talk about how easy it would have been if I hadn't sold the Range Rover, but I won't.

I felt the traffic slowing down to watch as I pushed her big grey arse past the gearstick. *Heeehaww heee-hawwww.* Conor McGregor grabbed her legs to stuff them into the back seat. We found a balance, with the passenger seat fully reclined, and the donkey's head up front with her chin on the dash. There was very little room for me, but the door closed with the donkey inside. The sanctuary on the northside was about thirty minutes of traffic away.

I said to the boy, 'What do you call her?'

'Susan,' he said.

I heard a voice behind me shout: 'Only in Limerick!'

It was a stubbly yob with his window rolled down, his grin lit up turquoise in the dark. He was recording me on an iPhone.

I wanted him to see a good man. A caring man. A man who took the time out of his evening, to stop and rescue a misfortunate abused donkey, at Christmas of all times.

'Only in Limerick?' Was this a joke to him? Did he think I was having a laugh?

The donkey and I crawled along Mulgrave Street as I fought the strain on the chassis. Driving became as physical as a cycle, the accelerator pushed back on my foot. The gearstick rattled and the metal undercarriage squeaked against tarmac. My chin was on the steering wheel. The donkey's heartbeat thumped against my spine like a Ronan Keating song. Her lagging jacket lungs heated the car and exhaled a dripping condensation that was pointless to wipe away.

You don't fully appreciate how large a donkey's head is until it's beside you in a Fiat Punto. The view in my mirror was furry and violent. I was driving blind. And the car took on a barnyard stink. That sugary blend of fresh shit and hay. There was powerful blast of cheese too. The elf's hat stapled to Susan's ear was tickling my face. A maggot from a sore dropped down on my jacket and I did gawks from the thought of fried rice. *Heeehawww heeehawww.* This was very difficult. But the suffering was necessary. I did not regret this decision. Even when the cars were overtaking me and beeping in frustration.

A business-looking man in a Beemer rolled down his window with a 'what the fuck are you playing at' face, but he never got them words out when his eyes met the donkey behind the foggy windscreen. He rolled the window back up because this was none of his business.

I tried to have a little cry, but it wouldn't come. It must have been the adrenaline.

I felt the ghost of my da's brain wibble inside my skull where my brain was. My father was the type of man who'd have rescued a donkey in his time. A vet he was. Who'd take his work home with the size of his heart.

He never ate meat. He would scatter bread out for robins when the ground was hard. Stepped over snails. Mouth-to-mouth on an epileptic rat. He'd draw a litter of kittens to the back door and put himself out of pocket feeding them.

Our childhood dog was a nervous lurcher called Flap who had a grin like a smashed seashell. He had crawled into the arse of an engine for warmth because the mange took his coat. A zombie-looking dog who'd frightened me. My da nursed the wiry fur back on to his gooey skin with love and patience. He would have been in this car with an abused donkey and not a fuck given towards what anyone else thought of it.

But this man was not the usurper above in St Camillus nursing home. Gums sloppy with sausage and black pudding from the fingers of a nurse. And him calling me a paedophile priest and a dirty pervert. This twisted new man who spoke about thumbs up arses and spit on tits, this sex man, who shat hatred and unfounded accusations at me whenever I'd visit. In September, he thought I was a brent goose and tried to repair my beak. I resisted, and he howled until an orderly would stick their head in the door like I was harming him. And the red face on me. This man who hated his son. That rude stranger.

'If I ever get that way, I want to be put down,' he said to me last year.

I turned to Susan and said: 'Do you think he took the bad turn because I couldn't afford the private nursing home any more? Did the shock of that cause the dementia knots to twist?'

And *Heehaaw heeehaw*, she replied, and the wound on her neck opened up. It winked pinky, shiny, and I felt her voice vibrate through my hands on the steering wheel.

The hot tears were forming behind my eyes, but they still wouldn't come. I thought about the video I'd seen online, where a squinty old American woman briefly regained her personality when they played her songs from her youth. She smiled at her daughters, and they smiled back.

'We haven't far to go,' I said to Susan, 'you'll have no worries in the sanctuary. They'll clean you up and you'll never be hit with a coat hanger again. No more selling Christmas trees. You'll frolic in a long garden with the other donkeys. Like a donkey heaven but you'll be alive. You're very lucky you met a kind man like me, Susan. I'll tell himself all about you. It might stir something up in him?'

She didn't respond, and her black pudding eyelids reminded me of my father above in his bed.

Susan, at what point do you accept that the person you love is dead, even though their body is still here?

The air of the northside tasted of the peat smoke bite that it gets in December. Toothy little tenements and Fanta orange clouds over a trolley in a ditch.

The woman who came to the gate of the donkey sanctuary had the face of someone who had forgotten whether they liked donkeys or not. I'd been expecting a different face, an 'aren't you a kind man for taking the time out to rescue a donkey and so close to Christmas' face.

We pulled Susan from the Punto and they cut off her green elf's hat with pliers, and replaced it with a plastic tag.

'Will ye find her a good home?' I asked.

'I dunno love, its face is half septic. The vet will decide what happens to it,' she said.

And Susan said *heehaw heehaw clop clop* as they walked her into a concrete pen.

The passenger seat of the Punto was fucked. Busted backwards on a permanent incline. There were no tears left at the bottom of me. I·did everything the way I was supposed to. I was selfless.

And this one evening, the evening with the donkey, I wondered to myself if my father would even notice if I ever went back to visit him.

The Pistils of the Dandelions

The tomcat's penis was barbed with backwards keratinised spines. This made the coitus incredibly painful for their mother. She had been in heat and mated with two other toms that day. This one had long white fur and different coloured eyes. His two front canines lodged into the marmalade tabby hair at the back of her skull. She howled an agonising wail. He withdrew and attempted to scrape out the semen of the previous male using his barbs. His efforts were not successful.

They were born under a purple morning sun. In a nest of styrofoam and rags assembled by their mother in a tarmac wasteland, against the back wall of a corrugated hardware store. The type of yellow land you see with the side of your eye. Between the retail parks. Where cars dump washing machines.

Brother and sister. Conceived by two different fathers. A rare thing but still natural within the superfecund reproductive system of cats. The female kitten came out a brilliant black, almost blue, with the tiger patterns of an orange tabby revealing itself across her belly. Her brother was born piss-yellow white, with a pink nose and pink little paws like his father. Their mother stretched her long orange torso in among the rags and licked her two new kittens clean. She gently nudged their faces towards her nipples to take her milk. They both fed voraciously. She mewed and rattled a gentle sound that was just for the comfort of her two small babies. Her paws flexed out and revealed ten sharp talons. She purred with great awe and pride at the two balls of fluff that she had just given birth to. Hidden among the nettles and dandelions in the styrofoam and polyester rags. A family. The kittens let out their tiny meows into the night against the whoosh of nearby cars.

On the first morning after their birth, a collection of crows were gathering near the wasteland. Peppering the horizon. They followed the rubbish trucks that serviced the hardware store. A raggedy black crow heard the mews of the two kittens and soon alerted the rest. Hungry for the sweet new organs and innards of day-old babies. Two flew down to where the kittens lay blind and helpless with their mother. The crows worked in pairs. One would hobble close to her, cawing, teasing, outstretching his black wings, drawing her out and distracting her, while his accomplice stalked her two kittens behind her back. She fought them off with a guttural ferocity. She swiped, hissed and spat. Directing attention at one crow, and then flipping back to attack the other. A frenzy overtook her. She arched her spine and her tail was electric with spiky fur. She found a roar in her belly that rumbled like a petrol lawnmower. The rest of the crows watched from atop a grey steel fence, some perched on the security cameras that were fixed to the green corrugate of the hardware store. All cawing, cheering, fanatic, hoping for a fresh meal. This was sport.

The two crows gave up, and the entire flock disappeared with slapping noises, flying off in search of the rubbish bins. The mother cat was too ferocious for them, too protective of her beloved new kittens.

Her heart beat fast and her energy was low from labour and producing milk. She returned to the nest to find that the little male had a scarlet stain on his white face. He was screeching out with his tiny toothless pink mouth open. One of the crows had tried to peck his eye while her back was turned. His eyes which had not even opened to the world. The mother licked his face in a panic. She cleaned away the blood with her tongue. She did this every single day to keep the wound clean.

The kitten and his sister fed at her teat. Their mother licked his eye at every opportunity. Caring for the bloodied area, helping it to heal. She had saved him from death, but after a week, as they opened, the injured eye scabbed and the eyeball was rejected by his skull. It hung brown and dry from his face, and so his mother licked it off and cleaned the socket. He had one blue eye; the other might have been green like his father's.

She continued to care for her kittens. Always watching them, vocalising, dedicating her every decision and movement to their survival. Now a few weeks old, with a spring in their jumps. The girl, fluffy and black with two green eyes. The boy with one eye was an ochre white. Playful and mewing. They nipped at their mother's heels. They followed her through the tarmac and the briars, over the broken glass, under the abandoned car at the far end. They pounced on rusted Coke cans, and dived at dandelion clocks, sending the fluff of the flower floating over the wasteland. Having only one eye, the male kitten would always miss his

target when he tried to pounce on a wasp or a butterfly. The female kitten would nip at her mother's
dangling teats while she walked, and the mother would
swipe and pin the kitten to the tarmac, with a firm but
gentle bite on her little throat. To let the kitten and
her brother know that they were getting too old for
her milk now.

The family cut a trail through nettles and would use
it to travel to the perimeter of the wasteland to feed
beside the iron fence. It was very common for hungry
cats to die from eating poisoned rats. They were slow
and easy to catch. So people would visit in the evenings.
To push paper bags through the fence and scatter dry
cat food in huge piles on the ground. Hordes of feral
cats depended on this. These feedings drew out all of
the stray cats in the nearby area. Different colonies and
groupings of cats with their own hierarchies. The sun
through the railings cast lanky blue shadows and it cut
across them all. Solitary cats who didn't belong to a
group always ate the food last. To break this rule meant
ferocious fighting.

She and her two kittens were solitary. She had never
settled with a colony, so the family would rummage
around the tarmac for itinerant brown nuggets with the
other lone cats. This took a lot longer than feeding

directly from the piles. But their mother didn't feel as nervous around humans as the other cats in the wasteland. She had the way of a cat that might have been close to a human at one point in her kittenhood. She was abandoned maybe. Let out of a car. It was too long ago. Occasionally, during the feedings, she would rub against the perimeter fence to the delight of the humans. She would meow like a kitten would, using an interspecies body language that she must have learned somewhere. It wasn't natural. A way of behaving that the other feral cats didn't possess. Those cats always kept a cautious distance from the humans on the other side of the fence, even when they held out food in their palms. A strict separation that wild animals understood as instinct. But when the orange tabby mother would rub against the fence, and mew like a kitten, a human would lay down food, for her and her kittens only. She would allow a hand to stroke her back through the metal. Her kittens learned to emulate this by watching their mother. This is when they got the best feeds, and it stood to them. It gave them a slight advantage during the evening feedings by the perimeter fence.

There wasn't much to be hunted in the wasteland. It was overgrown tarmac and concrete. Tufts of grass broke through in little islands. A few hawthorn shrubs sprang up here and there. It was mostly nettle, dandelion, thistle and dock leaf. Anything with a shallow root that could survive on moss or muck over stone. Spiderwebs would glisten between the grass at sunset. Hedgehogs or hares never got that far with all the cars. The lack of soil kept insect life to a minimum. The council sprayed weedkiller through the fence once a year, so everything was bleached yellow around the edges – nothing had a chance. A mouse or a shrew hadn't much business in there. Nowhere to burrow, no invertebrates to eat. The retail park beside the wasteland was no place for rats either. The hardware store kept Rentokil on hire 24/7, laying out poison and traps. A rat hadn't been seen there in years. A fox might pass through the fence, sniff the air and leave. Other than that, just the odd pigeon or crow. Staying safe high on the fences, electrical wires and corrugated roofs overhead.

But there were plenty of cats in the wasteland. Hundreds of cats a day, mostly belonging to the colonies, skulking across, marking territory. Toms fighting, the ammonia spice of their piss hovering low, basking if there was a bit of sun. But no hunting to speak of. This was dead ground in the wasteland.

The small kittens still pounced on anything that moved. Living or dead. An ant, a crisp packet bothered by a breeze. Their mother's eyes were sharpened to this. Even with the full belly from the feedings by the perimeter fence. The hairs on her ears would prick up at the sound of a smaller animal. It was this instinct that brought her to the hawthorn bush. The one that grew out from disturbed tarmac beside the abandoned car. The rust fed it iron in the soil, so its bark was blood red. It was larger than the others, about seven-foot tall with dense spiny branches and thick olive leaves.

The melody of a blackbird had been filling the wasteland in the mornings. It was a male who sang. Slick black feathers and a chest that gloated when he whistled. And there was a quieter female who had built a small nest at the top of the hawthorn bush. Nuzzling and proud, continental quilting her chicks with a bright citrus beak and eyes like drops of ink. He sang every morning and evening, to announce his territory, to protect his mate and their babies in their nest. He sang about taking care of his family.

The mother cat and her kittens had been sniffing and searching around the hawthorn. She could hear the blackbird above her. But the hawthorn was too treacherous to climb, with sharp spines on the branches.

A native bird in a native tree. This was a natural defensive structure for a blackbird's nest. She attempted it, but decided not to climb any further in case she became injured or trapped.

For three days she stalked the hawthorn bush. Whenever she heard the chirpy song. Laying low with her belly stuck to the tarmac. Wiggling her backside. Her kittens did the same, watching their mother hunt. When the blackbird would sing, her eyes would fix upward with a mania in them, pupils blossoming into black circles, and her mouth became possessed – her gums would rattle and clack, making a rapid *eck eck eck* noise, as if she was impersonating the bird to call it down.

On the fourth day, demented from his song, she heard a tiny chirp under the hawthorn, among the thickets of coarse grass and nettles adjacent the rusted car. It was a baby blackbird who had fallen from the nest. Flicking its neck and jittering the green blades of grass. Its large grey head and strange skin-covered eyes, jerking like a leather puppet, screaming for its mammy with a yellow mouth. The cat dived on the tiny bird and held it between her lips. It wriggled excitedly under her chin. She walked high on the pads of her paws with her head up as she delivered the hatchling to her kittens. The black kitten pounced on the bird first. Leaping playfully, pounding and mashing her paws on the little body. Gumming her teeth around its face. Standing on her hind legs with her tail stabilising her torso. *Cheap chip cheaaaap.* Coming down. Swiping with her paw, and the bird's featherless wing stuck in her small claws. Her claws like needles. She tried shaking the bird off her paw as if her paw was wet. Driven by a curiosity about killing, but not understanding how to do it.

The two blackbirds watched silently from atop the hawthorn while the kitten used their baby for practice. A cruel, slow and drawn-out procedure. The animal didn't die from any one wound or piercing, it died from the shock of it all. The cats didn't eat the bird.

The orange tabby then directed her attention to her male kitten who had yet to toy with the bird. His white shoulders were turned towards his mother and sister. The mother mewed to get his attention; he didn't move, his pink ears didn't cock, so she slowly walked over to him. He was staring off in a different direction, his one blue eye focussed on a bumblebee around a thistle. He was becoming deaf. The same as his father. An affliction common to cats with white coats.

Once his mother nudged him, he turned his head and saw his sister with the dead hatchling. His pupils dilated. He lay low, wiggled his bum, and floated up into the air to pin the bird. He crashed down on his sister instead and tumbled against an old glass Lucozade bottle. It rattled and the blackbirds screeched. When he tried to play with the dead bird, it was awkward. He didn't possess depth perception and his swipes missed. The corpse kept tormenting him while his mother and sister stood back and watched. Shadows lengthened and the air got colder. One by one, flies began to buzz around the little bird's wounds and crows perched on the electrical lines overhead. The blackbird sang a new song. The mother moved her two kittens on. The white one followed behind his sister.

Two months passed and the kittens were meowing less. They had less need to call for their mother to transport them in her mouth by their necks. They were maturing. Teenagers. A wild adult cat does not meow; wild adult cats are silent. Meowing is dangerous. The wasteland wouldn't allow them to adapt to the state of perpetual kittenhood that an adult domestic cat enjoys when it mimics the cries of a human baby.

The mother and her kittens continued their regular routine of visiting the wasteland perimeter fence to feed in the red evenings. The colonies of other cats would arrive too. The *whoosh* of kibble flowing from a paper sack. Mews and cacks. Fast paws shuffling dirt. Silence. The wet of mouths crunching on cat food. Occasional scuffles and roars. The laughs and chatting of the people who brought the food.

The kittens were older, larger, with proper-sized heads, looking a bit like all the other cats but delicately thin and still manoeuvring their limbs with the rubbery chaos of baby cats. Their mother's trick of charming her fur against the fence wasn't as effective now. The humans were much more receptive to her when she had two small kittens. Now they ignored her meows. And they didn't like the scrawny white cat with one eye. He looked like he had something contagious, they all agreed. They were repelled by that fear of growing fond of something that might die soon. So the orange tabby and her family would wait for the colony cats to finish and feed on what was left with the other loners.

Back around the styrofoam nest, they would fight with each other more frequently. Daughter and mother would arch their backs, drool, lick their lips, hiss, lash out claws. Cling together in a violent ball and send fur in the air. Thudding against the corrugated metal wall of the hardware store. All three of them were hungry all of the time because there was less food to go around. The brother and sister had developed larger appetites. They would search around the hawthorn tree, but the blackbirds had gone. The white cat was visibly thinner than his sister. His eyesight made him far less adept at spotting a nugget of kibble in the tarmac.

They didn't venture beyond the wasteland. The strong scents of the different colonies laid out a confusing and dangerous map. Too much data to navigate. Too many rivalries in too small an area. It was safest to stick to their area. Stay within the perimeter fence.

It was the heat of summer with no rain having fallen for two weeks. This made the asphalt bubble, and the whole place stank of tar. One day two boys of about ten or twelve passed through the wasteland. They had climbed over the perimeter fence. They searched around the tarmac for glass bottles, which they then smashed against the abandoned car near the hawthorn tree. The noise alerted the mother, who pricked her ears up and skulked by a patch of grass to watch the boys from a safe distance. Her two shadows followed behind. Sniffing the air. Their bellies met their spines, they were thirsty. They ate butterflies when they caught them.

The mother paused her step and threw a firm look behind her shoulder. Her kittens stayed back and hid in the grass. She decided to get closer to the two boys.

'Pss psss pss,' said the taller of the two boys.

She rubbed against his leg, purring, moving around in circles with her tail up high and shaking the tip like a snake. Nudging her wet muzzle into his empty palm for food. The boy stroked her neck gently, she raised her chin, and he ran his hand down her back. She purred more for him, and then salivated. She was initially reluctant, but something about a human stroke felt familiar and safe to her. It had worked before. He then grabbed her by the scruff and held her out with his arm stretched, pointing her at the other boy.

'This is how they carry their kittens, man. Like this, watch. When you grab them like this behind the neck, they go paralysed. It's a trick that the mothers have to move the kittens around,' he said.

He held her up, towards the high midday sun. Her body was stiff, eyes in a squint and her face was taut, with his fist gripping firmly at the marmalade fur on the back of her head. You could hear her breathing loud from her nose as her torso dangled and cast a small round shadow over the rust.

The boy then swung her body down on the bonnet of the abandoned car. This let out a dead thud. She bounced to the ground, frozen by the daze in her brain. Before she could feel the adrenaline to escape, the other boy raised a large rock over his head, and with both hands brought it down on her back, just above her orange tail. Breaking her hind leg and shattering ribs. There was no screech because it winded her. She lay beside the car, unable to move, making a strange licking movement with her tongue between low howls. The asphalt wobbled metallic under the hot sun. The usual city hum was quietened by the daytime heat. The boys paced around the wasteland. Nervous and excited. Spitting. Kicking things. Not letting the other see any fear or shock at what they'd just done.

The taller boy then left the wasteland by squeezing through the fence near the back of the hardware store. The other sat on the bonnet of the abandoned car and took out a cigarette. He tried puffing smoke into rings. He wasn't very good at it, so he made a fish-mouth shape with his lips and tapped the side of his cheek. Smoke chugged out in intervals and expanded into white circles against the squinty sky. While focussing up through a ring, he fixed his eyes on the overhead electrical wires. He returned to the mother cat who had managed to hide some of her body under the car. She was wheezing with foamy sputum dripping from her nose to the tarmac. Black ants drank from its edges. She produced a husky howl that rattled, a bubbling sound in her lungs when she inhaled. The howl was for her kittens. Her cry reverberated up through the metal of the car which made it louder and more hollow sounding. The boy paused to listen to this with curiosity.

He then pulled her out from under the car by her back legs. And remembering something he'd seen an older boy do with a cat before, he swung her body up towards the power lines. Hoping that he would see sparks or an explosion. But he wasn't strong enough. Each time, he failed and missed the power line by a few feet. Her body would spin down horizontally like a heavy sycamore seed and land with a thud on the tarmac below. He tried this four times then gave up.

The taller of the two boys returned. He had been in the hardware store, and had stolen a bottle of fluid with a red cap. They emptied the bottle on to the mother cat, who was still alive, and then set her on fire. She died screaming. The boys tried to kick her body under the hawthorn to set it on fire. But it didn't work; too much sap in the bark to catch ablaze.

The black kitten could hear the howls. Even though she was maturing, she still possessed the instincts of a baby. She felt danger and remained perfectly still in the grass, undetectable, waiting for her mother to collect her. Silent. Her brother could not hear anything and had wandered off in the opposite direction on the trail of a cooling breeze.

The sky had darkened with the promise of rain. Turning the air navy blue. Summer clouds that make green things seem greener.

'There's its kitten,' said the taller of the boys, seeing the little white dot on the other side of the wasteland.

The male kitten was in an open area of tarmac and his bright fur made him stand out from the green and the grey. He was curled up and resting. The tall boy moved towards him. The shorter boy, in a pang of guilt, threw a stone at the kitten to frighten it away. It landed, but he didn't hear it. As the tall boy got closer and could make out the size and shape of the cat, he rose up on his toes and crept, careful not to disturb the broken glass under his feet, but there was too much glass in the wasteland and it crunched and cracked.

The noise made the sister very uneasy. The instincts of an adult cat surfaced up in her. The hunger to escape in a flurry. She burst out from the grass she'd hid in and ran past the boy. Darting away like a tadpole in a sudden shadow. A dark blur. She swept past her brother's nose, and he felt the wind of her tail. He followed her because following her was all he had known. They both scarpered under the perimeter fence. Beyond the wasteland and past the hardware store. Across the motorway. Two black and white smudges. Through wooden fences. Under the barks of dogs. Him following her every gallop. And fat drops of cooling rain pounded the earth and asphalt and drummed on the corrugated roofs of the retail park. Serious puddles. Tarmac shone like leather, weeds stiffened, gutters slushed and gurgled with violent brown water, and everything everywhere smelled like hidden oil.

The rain stopped and steam wisped up from the footpaths. They settled on a mowed lawn where the air carried the freshness of trees but still had the hum of cars and people. They kept silent and rigid with the confusion. Separated from their mother for the first time. The sun cracked out of a cloud and lay a warming marmalade beam across their faces, then went away. Under a sycamore, the white cat curled his tail around his paws and lifted up his neck, his one blue eye in a squint and his nostrils inflating and contracting. He bobbed his head and studied the air. His sister purred and rubbed against him from behind. He flinched. They pressed their foreheads together and rubbed noses. There was nothing familiar on the gust. The torrents of rain had washed away any smell of the wasteland. No marking or trail from a tom survived. Their maps were wiped. Nothing could lead them back. They lived among the houses now.

It came into autumn. The suburbs were quiet. Semi-detached houses with terracotta roofs over ample back gardens. Winding roads and grassy parks with trees. Alleys for creeping behind the houses. Gentle breezes that told stories about cats, dogs, bins, foxes, bats. The comforting perfume of flower beds over freshly cut lawns. Dark pools of ponds with fat golden carp swimming in a hypnotic circle that kept their necks manic. The song of the swallow and robin. There was a new map of smells to crack. The markings of house cats were less definite than in the wasteland. These odours didn't speak about murder. They would follow their noses along the trails and find the feeding dishes of these domestic cats.

There was no shortage of cat food in the suburbs either. Spilling out of ceramic bowls at back porches, inside cat houses. Wet food. Cans of oily mackerel. She would even steal food from the bowls of dogs. And she would always go first. Hopping up on a back wall and surveying the garden. Making sure it was clear. They had their favourite spots.

He would follow her. It always took him longer. Everything took him longer. To jump up on a wall, he had to stare up and study the ledge. Wiggling his white arse. Focussing the pupil of his eye, dilating it, trying his absolute best to correctly gauge the distance before springing forth with the muscles of his back legs. A fierce long leap. It didn't always work, and he'd miss the tops of walls, bouncing his chest off the edge and winding himself. Or he'd tear his claws into breeze block concrete, dangling, dragging himself up. He would howl while doing this. He hadn't much self-awareness when it came to noise due to his deafness.

The cats were maturing into adulthood now, ready for the next spring. She had become strong and healthy. Her thick, beautiful black fur bunched around her neck and the tabby pattern of her mother came through her belly in orange bands under sunlight. Her oval eyes were bright lime green. Her coat slick and teeth healthy from the endless supply of fish and Whiskas that she stole from the bowls of house cats who didn't really care. No end to the licking and grooming. And she was completely silent. Clean with no smell. Always skulking low, avoiding humans, and moving invisibly against the night time. Soft pads under the paws, not a chirp out of her.

But her poor ould brother's coat was unkempt and raggedy. Yellowed white like a sheep. Limp pink ears that didn't cock. The continual stress and confusion of being deaf and one-eyed had written itself into the expression on his face. His mouth was frightened and full of caution. His single beautiful azure eye consistently widened in alertness. His chin stained brown. He was clumsy. He followed his sister to food, but ate last and often alerted a human or a dog who would chase him away before he finished.

He developed two awkward white testicles that dangled between his back legs and jutted out so you'd see them from the side. He began to mark the walls and gardens of the suburbs with the shake of his tail and backside. A noxious blinding ammonia tang, which then attached to his fur. His forever state of stress had him grooming less and less. You could smell him before you saw him. He yawed and mawed in the alleyways between the houses in the dead of night. Dying for a mate.

Feral tomcats would wander into the suburb by the strength of his markings and the smell of his sister in heat. They would search for him and attack. He would try to fight back but was outmatched by the stronger, faster males. His ferocious sister would fight his corner instead. Swiping, hissing, arching her spine and latching in a ball on any cat who came for her brother. Then he would try to mate with his sister.

It was this antisocial behaviour that had them trapped by the rescue people. There was a chimney smoke moon above an alley in the winter when they both caught wind of cooked chicken that was wafting in the air. The chicken was bait and they found themselves locked in a plastic cage together. Torches blinding their faces. Gloved fingers pressing around their gums. He howled and she kept as quiet as she could while thumping in the box to escape. Tearing the heads off each other.

Trapped with blankets and pinned to a stainless-steel vet's table. The terrifying milky stink of humans all over their bodies. Because they were feral, no attempt was made to find them a home. They had gone beyond the point of domestication. They were both neutered and released back into the suburb. When they spayed her, the vet removed the foetuses of three kittens.

They were a year and a half old now. They both had little fat pockets that dangled under their bellies. They spent more time lounging and stretching. You'd think they were domestic by the shape of them. The white cat had become incredibly docile. He didn't mark any more, he didn't howl, and was happy to trail behind his sister. There was no more fighting other than the occasional swipe and hiss between siblings. They had found a home in one of the houses in the suburb that was unoccupied by people. A garden in the rear that was overgrown and full of nettles like the wasteland. It was protected by high walls, no person or animal ever ventured in, and they slept in an old tool shed that was falling apart. It was shelter, nonetheless. It kept them dry from rain and away from winds. Everything felt safe, the air had no warnings in it, and they had no reason to leave the garden.

On one of those mornings where the grass was crystal white and crunched with frost, she was jarred from sleep by the sound of movement in the garden. Her brother did not hear. She poked an inquisitive black face out through a wooden slat in the busted shed. Ice powdered on her brow, and she flicked her two ears. A young woman was slowly inspecting every corner and crevice of the garden. The woman's arms were folded high on her chest and her breaths were cornflower blue against the dead winter. The black cat nudged her brother and they both quietly exited the back of the shed.

The two cats observed the woman from the safety of the breeze block wall while she gently moved old flowerpots over with her wellies and tugged at the loose slats of the shed. She hummed a Mariah Carey song. She had long brown hair and a softness to her voice. She arched her neck up and spotted the black cat and white cat who were surveying her. She gasped like a child, paused a bit and blinked her eyes slowly in a secret cat-human language.

'Pss pss pss,' she said to them, with her hand out, rubbing her fingers together.

The cats kept a cautious distance and watched with no discernible emotion from atop the wall. The sister sat tall and proud with the tail wrapped around her two feet and the tip wagging slow, and himself behind her looking on with one eye and his sad mouth. Peering down on the woman nonchalantly, as if they were to be worshipped.

The woman walked off with brisk excitement and soon came back, trying to woo them both with a slice of ham in her palm. Lifting it up above her head towards the top of the wall. They could smell the delicious meat, but still refused to let her get close. Consistently backing away as soon as she got near to them. She gave up.

Later that evening the woman returned, and placed an entire can of tuna by the back door.

'Pss psss pss,' she said towards the tool shed.

The two cats waited with caution until she had gone back inside. Herself silent, himself smelling the air and mawing. And then they had a fine feed. A frenzy of licking and smacking afterwards. The pink of his mouth on display and the little hairy tongue searching every millimetre of his muzzle for a bit of missed tuna. The black cat held up her paw and using her head, rubbed vigorously all around her ears and scalp. Giving herself the perfume of fish oil. As if to let any other cat know how well she was doing for herself. The woman watched all of this from the kitchen window with a proud smile on her face. Thrilled that she had brought happiness to the two fur babies out in her new back garden.

'They'll keep coming back if you do that,' the man said.

'This is their house,' she said, 'they live in that shed out there. We've moved into their house. It's us who are their guests.'

He wrapped his arms around her waist and they both stared at the animals. Awestruck and free from worry, hypnotised by their behaviour.

'That poor little white one with the eye is cute,' he said.

The tuna turned into Whiskas and bowls of milk. The food became regular. Once in the morning and once in the evening. A predictable routine. Just like in the wasteland of their youth. But there was no competition now. This was all for them. They were safe. They were warm. They were fed.

Their days were spent rolling around in the grass and letting the sun hit their bellies. Their biggest concern was finding the most comfortable position to rest in. The shed had been knocked down, and a small wooden cat house was built for them with a soft foam bed inside. They slept together for warmth. She licked her brother's fur and kept his neck clean. They purred and kissed with noses. Growing older together.

His eyesight and his deafness were less of an issue in the garden. He'd occasionally pounce on a bee and crash into a flowerpot, leading to howls of laughter from the kitchen. The couple grew fond of the cats. Watching their antics from the window. Slow blinking and getting slow blinks back. But the cats in their wildness would still flinch and move away if the couple tried to pet them.

Two years passed and the suburbs were changing. The older residents were gradually being replaced by younger people. Ponds were filled in. Some gardens were razed and carpeted with sterile bales of plastic grass. Decking was built. In the garden, the grass stood tall and the shrubs gave shelter. The couple were cautious not to interfere with the little habitat that the cats had discovered.

'We'd be like colonisers,' she'd say.

But no matter how much food they provided, or how many slow blinks or 'pss psss' they could deliver, they couldn't establish a bond with the animals. For the cats it was a relationship of tolerance, and for the couple it was one of longing.

'I wish they'd let me pet them,' she'd say to him. 'Look at her beautiful coat. If only they didn't have to sleep outside either. They could sleep on the couch in here if they weren't so frightened all the time.'

'I'd love that too, it can get freezing out there,' he said back. 'But they're terrified of us.'

One evening the woman squeezed gelatinised cat food from a metal packet into a bowl. She had been busy that morning and missed a feed. She used both hands to make sure all of the jelly made it to the dish. The aroma of chicken and beef wafted through the air. As her fingers pressed on the foil, she noticed the photograph of the cheerful domestic cat on the design. The black cat was particularly hungry and began to feed immediately without keeping her usual distance.

The woman spotted an opportunity and reached her hand forward. She gently rubbed her finger on the black cat's forehead between her eyes. The cat hissed immediately. She didn't understand this physicality. She had no frame of reference for this touch. It was an attack. She jumped, and waited for the woman to go back inside. Her brother stood behind her.

But as her brother grew stronger with the regular food, and the stress of his life eased, he developed an independence. He followed his sister less and found a personality for himself. His face softened; he lost the look of fear and the sad mouth.

When the man sat out to enjoy the garden with his coffee, the white cat would slowly walk closer and lie down beside him. The man began to carefully unfurl his arm and rub the cat's soft white paw, eventually moving his fingers towards the plush fur of his neck. The white cat purred for him, and closed his one eye. Stretching his chest out and relishing the scratches and affection. The woman would do the same, stroking her hand down his fluffy white belly that he pointed at the sky. The black cat would stand back at a safe distance at all times. Watching. Confused. Forever on alert. Always silent. Her brother began to meow when he saw the couple in the mornings. Rubbing off their legs, pouncing up with enthusiasm, purring like an engine and demanding his breakfast, to the delight of the couple. Behaving like his mother in the wasteland when she begged for food from the people at the fence.

Soon, the male cat would walk in the back door, through the kitchen, and explore all over the house whenever he pleased. Upstairs into empty beds. Lying on windowsills. Purring and meowing. He would sleep between the couple up on the couch on chilly nights. The TV turned up full blast, making no difference to him. Curled up in a white ball. Stretching the talons. Yawning and getting little treats and rubs. Snoring in his sleep. Dreaming cat dreams that made his muzzle cack and his paws flick while the couple marvelled over him. His one eye and his snowy face glowing different colours from the light of the TV screen. Delighted with himself. His sister stayed outside in the cold. Watching it all in the window. They had given up on coaxing her into the warmth that her brother enjoyed.

Both cats were well looked after in the garden, but the white cat became the favourite. The couple took pity on him. They called him Sullivan because of the one eye. She didn't get a name. He was receptive to affection and rubs. He gave love back. He ate first now. In a separate dish that was in the kitchen near the bins. She ate outside.

Still, he was never fully domesticated. The wildness was there. Spending some nights in the wooden cat house with his sister and others inside on the warmth of the couch. He had found a compromise that met his needs. Taught by his mother who knew the touch of people. His sister stayed feral and cautious.

After years of comfort, the brother and sister found themselves in old age. Her muscle tone softened among the black fur and her spine, which was once a proud arch, slumped down and ended in a bent tail. Silver hairs grew above her eyes and grooming became more difficult. He was slow and round with problems in his bones. His walk was a style of hobble that he puffed out between sleeps. And the single blue eye faded into a cloudy grey that might bring a cataract. But they were adored and fed and sheltered.

It was a warm summer evening with long shadows when the couple brought the baby home. Butterflies and dandelion fluff floated through the blood-eyed sun, and the cats stuck their sweaty bellies to the sky to catch the last of it. The newborn was a soft pink lump of skin and cotton like a wobbling rose. Nestled in a pram in the kitchen. The couple stared into the cot with mad smiles on their faces. Intoxicated with disbelief at the confusing wonder of life. No external sensation could distract them. They lifted the baby up and took turns rocking it. Laughing. They squealed and mewed at their baby and the baby squealed back.

The cats would stare in the kitchen window at it all. Ignored. The white cat would meow and purr. The couple didn't come to his calls any more. A day or two might pass and their dishes went empty. The 'pss pss' stopped, no more slow blinks every morning or bits of ham. The woman would rush to the bins in the back garden with bags of nappies and step over the two cats. They'd scarper out of the way. The grass was replaced with plastic grass for when the baby could crawl. The uniform green spikes jutted into their skin and didn't cool them during that hot summer. They slept less. They began to bicker and hiss at each other again. Conditions worsened over the months. The baby cried out at night time and the noise kept the black cat on edge. All routine had changed in the garden.

Hungry and annoyed, the white cat strolled into the kitchen – he'd had no breakfast that morning. His tail in the air, cocky, the blue eye squinting and the pink mouth open. Meowing loudly. Calling for his humans. He carefully climbed up on to the kitchen counter by pulling himself up on a stool. Expending much more energy than he was used to. He licked crumbs of cheese from the surface. The baby was sleeping in the pram adjacent the counter. Wrapped up and warm.

The baby lay level to him, and he spotted her hands reaching up from her blankets. His meows had stirred her. The cat sniffed the air and was inspired by a curiosity for this little creature and its new smell. He arched himself at the edge of the kitchen counter to inspect closer. Four cotton ball paws stuck together, poised on the ledge. Stabilising his tail and wiggling his bum. Squinting his eye at the pram. His pupil like a full moon. Cocking his chin. Slow, considered. Trying to gauge the distance.

He leapt forward with his fat white torso stretched out, suspended for a moment in mid-air, before missing the pram spectacularly. To save his fall, one of his paws latched on to the side of the pram, talons out, the other found its way on to the baby's soft peach arm, leaving a long scratch. Young scarlet blood bubbled from each claw track on her skin. The wounds puffed. The baby screamed in pain. The white cat dangled. His spiky tail thrashing pointlessly like an extra limb. The weight of his body pulled the pram to the ground and the helpless infant rolled on to her front.

She couldn't lift her head up. Her nose pressed against the tiled floor. Crying, gasping, wailing with tiny pearls of red dripping from her skin. Her arms wiped out with each scream and stained the tiles in an arc. A little blood angel with one wing. Her pink knitted blanket falling off her. Her impossibly small body exposed. The white cat sniffed her cuts and licked the blood. The couple burst into the kitchen.

The man shouted, 'He's fucking attacked her, Jesus Christ.'

The white cat could not hear this. The man kicked the cat as hard as he could in the stomach, sending him flying across the kitchen. He escaped out the back door to the safety of the garden, mawing, falling over his feet, not understanding what had just happened. The couple hugged and held their howling baby between them. Rocking together like trees in a breeze. The woman and the man both cried in terror and relief.

Later that evening there was a cat carrier in the back garden where the black cat's food dish usually lay. Inside were two bowls of fresh tuna and milk. A rare feast. Even though she was hungry, the black cat kept her distance. Refusing to enter the carrier. Her brother saw no issue and hobbled into the box. He devoured the tuna for them both. When he turned to leave, the grate of the carrier had closed. She remained beside the carrier all night while her brother mawed inside. His one eye squinting. He did a pee and his feet slipped in the wet plastic as he tried to escape. She paced. She rubbed against the carrier. Trying to kiss noses through the wire.

In the morning, the man appeared. He hissed at her loudly and kicked the ground, sending a flowerpot in her direction. It crashed violently. She clambered up the back wall and sat there in silence at a safe distance. She watched as the man walked off into the kitchen with the handle of the carrier in his fist. This was the last time she saw her brother.

She returned to the garden after a few hours and pressed her nose in the empty space near the kitchen door. Her cat house and her bed were no longer there. Sitting in the wet dark rectangle where she and her brother had slept for many years. Hundreds of wood-lice crawled around her paws. Her food dish was gone. She sniffed at nothing and remained silent and still. Sleeping with her black tail around her nose on the concrete by the door. The cold penetrating up through her withered limbs, the wind ruffling her neck and waking her up.

Occasionally the woman would open the window and hiss at her, while holding her baby. The man threw a mug of water at the black cat while she slept in a ball by the door. This was very frightening and unex-pected. After some weeks she left the garden.

Hungry, delirious and unsure. She would raise her

head and study the air in search of trails, but her senses had dulled in later years. The smells confused her. She travelled from house to house, but there were fewer cats in the suburbs with food dishes to steal from. She no longer had the stamina to scale walls and avoid dogs. Through the alleyways, she walked along on sore pads, slower now, pausing every so often. The muscles of her shoulders had memorised the movement of looking behind to check on her brother. This was the first time in her life that she had been alone.

The black cat found herself in an electrical substation behind an industrial estate. It was a maze of large grey metal boxes, with pathetic green sproutings of life occasionally breaking through mulch. Huge steel pylons towered above. This wasn't new to her. There were fewer smells than in the wasteland where she was born, but the dandelions and broken glass felt familiar and safe.

She stuck to walls and fences and picked up the trail of an animal. Through nettles a scent of urine revealed itself. She clung to it like a ball of string. Brushing against the grey metal box of an electrical substation. The cat stopped. It was a rat. Huddled in a ball like it was trying to stay warm. A light drizzle made everything electric hum and fizzle. She lay low and approached the rat from the side. The ground was a grey pebble mulch that had been laid to keep weeds from growing. No matter how much she softened her pads, the stones clacked loudly against the electrical buzzing. Slow movements. Her focus sharpened around the rodent so that nothing else existed in that moment. With each crunch under her paw she stopped, her body frozen, expecting the rat to hear her and dart off. But the rat was in a daze. Huddled and dumb. It didn't sniff the air or rub its face or hear her pounce. She dispatched the animal quickly with her teeth and devoured its guts. Satiated, she took shelter in a thicket of shrubs that jutted out from the substation wall. Strong smells of foreign toms wafted in. She curled up with her nose over her paws. The marmalade glow of a street light slithered through the leaves and speckled her black fur.

Convulsions and pains dragged her from her sleep. Her torso curled and unfolded with the tension of a stubborn spring. She struggled to breathe. A red foam dripped from her nose and stained the pebbles and her paws. She huddled in a ball like the rat she had eaten.

When she felt the final painful breaths of death, she began to meow like a tiny kitten. The O-shaped cries of a newborn filtered through adult lungs. She cried for her mammy to come and collect her.

And all of them, mother, brother and sister, melt into sludge and rise again in the pistils of the dandelions.

St Augustine's Suntan

The jackdaws build their nests in the confessional boxes of the deconsecrated Augustinian cathedral. I come here in the mornings to feed them petrol station sausage rolls. A teenage-looking jackdaw pecks at the pink of the sausage meat that I've thrown on the dusty tiles. Pig steam rising to his beak. He watches me watch him.

And then it begins, with these twenty-five very specific words in the following order: 'I want to tear the thoughts from the inside of my head and throw them splattered in a hedgerow ditch for the weasels to eat.'

I hear it as an inner monologue, in my own voice. Just them words, no imagery, because I can't imagine what it would look like for a weasel to eat one of my thoughts. But the words jut out from all my other words with their confidence.

My posture improves, my brow unfurrows. I feel

like a real person. There's no doubt around the agenda or self-sabotaging notions that someone else might do it better, or sneer at me if I tried. I want to tear the thoughts from the inside of my head and throw them splattered in a hedgerow ditch for the weasels to eat.

At the very core of me is a badness that I can't put words on. A feeling that I have done something terrible, and it is only a matter of time before I'm found out and punished. The thing is, I know that I haven't done anything bad. I've recounted every misdeed and wrongdoing. At first with priests and then with therapists. A dirty frying pan hasn't been scoured as much. No past action accounts for the wicked and persevering sourness at my heart.

I'm not the only one who returns here to this cathedral. Even though I've never seen another person, I notice their traces. The holy water font where I used to bless myself always has the new rusty turd of an adult man in it. It's not a dog or a fox that does it, because a dog couldn't get their arse up that high. It's a man, and he returns here to do it for his own reasons. There's a lonely plinth where a four-foot Padre Pio once stood with his blood gloves, and if you look closely, you will see the recurring print of an Adidas runner. I don't know whose it is, or what they do on the plinth, but they do it regularly.

This is a skeleton's church and there's holes where the windows were, and addicts do fentanyl in the crypts under the altar when there's moonlight. There's solid red wax splatters on the floor in the shape where the candle box was. The paint layers on the walls tell you where the crucifixes hung. You can try to remove all the religious iconography from a cathedral, pretend it's just an old building, blow out the ears and eyes of God, but something else will fill that space. Something that was there in the ground before the church. People come back here to perform their own rituals now. Memories burn into churches like a farmer's suntan. This is where I did my confessions as a child, in those boxes yonder, where the jackdaws nest. There's a healing here for me that I can't yet hear.

I first started seeing the priests when I was seven years old. I say seeing, but you never saw them during confession. Myself and my classmates would queue up in the slimy pews over there. Back then, around 1992, this was where everyone in my school visited when training for Communion and confession. There was the vinegar smell of radiator-dried-jumper rain in the ceiling over us. The dangly wet stalactite things, hanging from the rafters like they'd drop into your mouth. We'd point and say that they were fake sins that never made it up past the roof, so they just stuck there like melted ghosts. I'd be sconcing down at the floor tiles and thinking hard about what sins I might have committed before it was my turn. It was an urgent feeling, like I had lost something very important belonging to someone else, and I had to find it in a short amount of time.

With the little green head on me, the confession box had the look of two upright coffins nailed together with a hole in the middle. There was the hum of eternity inside the box. The timber would suck time out of the air and hold it in the walls. You'd breathe it in slow motion. The priest sitting limp behind a plywood gauze so that God could listen in with his huge ears like an inside-out Santa Claus.

You couldn't go to confession with no sins. So I'd plunder the past few months of my young skull for anything bad I'd done. Did I say any bad words? Did I steal a pound from my mother's purse? Did I get angry with her? Nothing. I wasn't much for sinning as a child to be honest. So long as I had cartoons or an ice cream, I was grand.

But you'd practise your sins with the teacher, Mrs O'Sullivan, before real confession with a priest, and she told me that liking ice cream and cartoons wasn't a big enough sin. I told her they were more or less all I thought about, to the point that it qualifies as a sin. Mrs O'Sullivan would urge me to remember a better sin so I didn't disgrace her in front of Father Sexton.

'All of us sin,' she said, telling me that I had the miserly sins of someone who's withholding bigger ones. The priest would smell it off me.

'Listening to sins is his job,' she'd say.

So I confided that I couldn't tell the difference between the taste of ice cream wafer and Communion wafer. Mrs O'Sullivan said that was a brilliant sin to bring to confession. A very advanced sin concerning the miracle of transubstantiation. I had an Orangeman's tongue on me that couldn't taste the Lord.

'A big dirty Protestant tongue that's not fit to lick the blood of his wounds,' she said.

I'd never been given so much praise in front of the class. I was thrilled.

We were told that God could flick the pages in our brains like a phonebook. The sins are logged in there, just for him, in a language only he can read. The Divil could go blind if he tried to read the sins you write in your mind. The point of the confession was for God to clean you so that your insides weren't manky before you ate his son. So the worst thing you could do was withhold a sin from the priest during confession. Then you'd be lying to a priest in front of God and poor Christ would have to dissolve wrong in the filth of you. You had to tell the priest everything. My friend Aaron Costelloe had to tell the priest that he enjoyed watching his goldfish take shits, for fuck sake.

Sometimes, if I hadn't a sin to confess, I'd ask some-one else for a lend of their sins. Georgy Slattery threw a stone into his neighbour's dog's face until it needed a vet, and so I took that one for him. My thinking at the time was that I probably had done something bad, but forgot, so by confessing someone else's sin as my own I was balancing it out with God.

Before long, other youngflas would offload their sins on me, big sins like robbing from shops or stab-bing their baby brother's legs with a compass. But I began to feel guilty, by confessing to sins that weren't mine. So I started to do them, as a type of method acting, so that they would become real sins that I could confess. I would rob from the shop. I would wait by the playground, looking for a distracted mother with a toddler, and creep up to her unattended baby in a buggy and stab its little thigh with a compass until it gave up a single pearl of blood. Which you might think is sufficiently bad to confess, but I wasn't doing it out of badness – I was doing it so my sin wasn't a lie before God. The truth of it was that I hated doing these things. No matter how much I carried out the offences, these were not my sins. The intent to be cruel wasn't in me. They were other children's sins that I was performing on their behalf. Just like a soldier who is killing during war. It's not a real sin. I could trick the priest, but God knew that these were not my authentic sins. He wouldn't let them past the roof. They flew up and stuck to the ceiling and hung down all melty.

When I'd confess, the priest would give me penance, like saying 'Hail Mary' twenty times. I'd listen to the pause in the priest's voice for the bigger sins. He used to go all high pitched. Like he wanted to punish me himself. Like he wanted to withhold penance because what I'd done was so bad and wrong. But he couldn't do that. Because I had confessed, he had to give me God's forgiveness. Those were the rules.

Instantly clean, free from sin and guilt. No more nights spent awake, thinking over and over about what a terrible boy I was. The wiped slate. The lanky fingers of God reaching into my head and pulling out the sin and the earth-clod guilty roots with it. Gone from me. And then I'd eat his tasty wafer son as a small treat. There was a simplicity to it all that you could only sell to a child.

Sure, I can't go to confession now. Because I'm in my thirties, and it's foolish, and we know all about what the priests were up to. A man in a box who you tell secrets to and some beardy cunt in the sky cures you of the torment? How can I put any currency in that?

So I started to believe in therapists. With the rigour of the science of psychology. Attending therapy is a bit like confession but with the windows open and light coming in. There's more shame to therapy though. With confession you've to wait in line with all the other people getting ready to confess. Ye can see each other. Yere desire to be washed is out there in the open.

With psychotherapy you've to hide. You're separated from anyone else who has a battered head on them. You will never see another therapy client as long you attend therapy. The counsellor makes sure yere schedules don't clash. It happened to me once last year that I arrived early to a transactional analysis session just as a man in his forties with weathered eyelids was leaving his appointment. He was a rat the way he scurried. We made small terrifying eye contact, and in that moment I felt like the Divil decoding the book of sins inside his head.

Was he sexually abused, I asked myself, and that's why he's here?

It made me feel a bit superior I suppose, which was then followed by a burst of fear, because what if he thought I had been abused and that's why I was in therapy too? So I followed him to his car and told him that I knew what he was thinking, and I'd never been abused and still haven't figured out the reason why I'm attending therapy. The man started to cry. Therapy is dirtier than confession. And I felt like confessing the shame of having turned up early to therapy deliberately to see another person sneaking out the door. Ateing their discretion with no salt like a glutton. I wanted to tear the thoughts from inside my head and throw them splattered in a hedgerow ditch for the weasels to eat.

My first ever therapist was a woman by the name of Dr Deirdre Foy and she was big into her attachment theory. How they came about with the attachment theory is a wicked one. These scientists in the

1950s were raising baby monkeys in sterile cubicles, complete isolation: no siblings and, most importantly, no mother. And what do you think happened to the baby monkeys? They began tearing the hair from their skulls and biting into themselves. They were given enough food, enough water and warmth, but ultimately it didn't matter a fuck. Without the cuddles and reassurance from their monkey mothers they went stone mad with the agony. So the scientists made fools of the baby monkeys by constructing them false mothers from wire and wool. And they'd worship their wire mothers with the little eejit heads on them, confusing the fur for love and support. The infant monkeys needed love and comfort more than they needed food and water.

Dr Deirdre Foy told me that my innate feeling of badness exists because my mother left me crying for so long as a baby that I thought I was dying. And now anytime I feel any discomfort as an adult, I believe that I will die from abandonment because I deserve it. Stress transports me back to my cot, helpless and supine with a fat pissy nappy and no movement of my body except the jittery primal howls from my lungs. No concept of the future or anyone returning to help me. No mother, not even a false fur metal monkey mother.

'An infant's yelp is always directed inwards as blame,' she said.

That's the feeling of badness in my head that has me tormenting myself with guilt, she says. I told her that it sounds like how the priests would describe hell to me in confession. A terrifying feeling of separation and abandonment from the love of God.

'It's not the same,' she said.

Then I asked her, 'If I'm now consciously aware that the reason I feel like a rotten person is because I was left in my cot for too long, why can't I shake the feeling? Surely knowing this answer will solve the problem? Like confessing a sin.'

She said that my pain is rooted in a time before I learned to relate to the world using words and images, so talking or thinking about it is useless to my adult brain. But I should still try to hug myself as a child using self-compassion. I said this sounded like being born with original sin, from Eve eating a snake's apple in the Garden of Eden, and that I'd already been cured of that during baptism. She disagreed and said that original sin is a misogynistic construct which vilifies women's desires. The snake was another man's penis, and the apple was her womb. The concept of original sin keeps women obedient to men by positing cuckoldry as the greatest sin of all, which we can pass on genetically. My feeling of badness is my mother's fault, and not Eve's.

And so, after, I rang my mother from the car park and asked her if she abandoned me in my cot, and she said it was far from abandonment I was reared with, and tried to convince me that my therapist didn't tell me to go hug myself but told me to go fuck myself, and that's when I stopped seeing the attachment therapist.

As I recount these memories, I think about killing my mother with a screwdriver. I instinctively scan the church, and search for the Holy Mary statue for forgiveness. It's gone, of course. But I stare at the deep recession in the wall where her statue once stood. Full of bright green moss and fag butts. An empty concave, like someone had scooped an eye out of a skull.

I don't want to be too hard on my mother. My mother grew up in poverty on a farm in Donegal with no mother of her own, and when I was about the age of four or five, she would read me bedtime stories about animals. Like the fox and the hen, or Chicken Licken. She would interrupt these stories because they were unrealistic. And tell her own stories from her childhood about the knowing terror in a pig's snort before her uncle slit its throat, or how she accidentally broke a baby duck's neck by drying it with a towel.

The story that stuck out for me most was how she would watch the jackdaws circling lambs. They would hover in the sky, scanning for a newborn lamb who'd got separated from its mother. And they would eat only the soft eyes from its head, with it still alive, before flying off. The mother sheep would hear the lamb's yelping bleats, but it was too late, and all she could do was lick the bloody holes where its eyes had been. Though I had never seen this, the image of it in my head as a child was vivid and smelled like iron. I saw it through my mother's eyes. The lamb would survive with no eyes, and would never leave its mother's side, even when it grew to be a big sheep. But that rarely got to happen – someone always ate it first.

'A jackdaw will peck anything that's helpless and pathetic enough,' she said.

I would ask my mother if it was sad when the jackdaws ate the lamb's eyes, and she said no, because it meant her father would kill it and they'd have lamb for Sunday dinner.

Now I'm no fool, and I've read my psychology, so it's no surprise to me that my plan about tearing the thoughts from the inside of my head and throwing them splattered in a hedgerow ditch for the weasels to eat came to me when it did. I was watching a jackdaw eating a sausage roll, and I suppose a part of me wanted my head to be the sausage roll, and I suppose an even deeper part of me wanted to be the lamb getting the eyes eaten out of his head while my own mother watched it happen as a toddler.

Because if I'm being honest, the way she'd tell the story to me back then, I could tell it disturbed her; it felt like a strange wish that she had for me. Like, if my eyes were eaten out of my tiny head, then she could move on from the pain of the memory. And I suppose, I should have taken this new awareness to a therapist to be analysed. And I would have, were it not for that teenage jackdaw putting those words in my head.

It was my attachment therapist's insistence that I practise self-compassion with a younger version of myself that had me returning to this cathedral. To retrace my steps in the aisles before confession. To hold my own hand, and hug myself, and tell myself not to be stressing too much about sins. Because a child can't sin anyway. And I suppose, in case I was abused here and I can't remember.

Because that's what we all think, isn't it? If you've

looked at the news at any point in the last thirty years. We all had to be locked in boxes with the priests, didn't we? With the guilt and the terror of what we might have done? And them being the only ones who could cure us of it? I'd have done whatever the priest told me my penance was if it meant being clean. How am I to know what happened or didn't happen to me? Doesn't it get pushed into the unconscious mind to a place where words don't exist, like my therapist would say? Or what if it didn't happen to me? And it happened to my mother, and she passed it to me through the image of a baby sheep with bloody holes for eyes?

I was drawn here. Into this rotten building. The sausage rolls were just a bit of comfort. You could tell that God's long ears no longer pointed at the confession boxes – they didn't need to. There was nothing of any major interest to him in a jackdaw's mind, because there's too much honesty to them. They could never hide the complexity of a lie under that clacking beak. I've come to realise that the jackdaws are the priests of nature. Always watching, always reporting back. With their black chests and white-collared heads. It's no coincidence at all to me that they chose the confessional box as their nesting place. I've done my research.

In the old myths of the Leabhar Gabhála Éireann, the goddess Morrigan would appear as a jackdaw and manipulate events towards their natural conclusion.

Before confession, before Christ, before psychology, we had trepanation. When a pain was too great, or a disturbance too much to bear, our skulls were trephined. Either a hole was bored, or it was scraped with flint or obsidian. This would relieve pressure on the mind and allow the pain to escape. In school, we learned about the bog bodies with the holes in their heads that were found deep in the peat of the Shannon marshes.

I gently pull back the door of the confessional box. I brush away the sticks, shit and eggshells that scatter the little bench where I sat all those years ago. The wooden gauze the priest once sat behind is twined with bits of twigs and leaves. The smell of eternity still holds in the wood. Air passes into my lungs in slow motion. I take my last sausage roll from the hot tinfoil petrol station bag, place it gently on my head, and wait for an intervention.

A jackdaw appears, with his beady eye assessing me in an antiseptic way. He leaps up on to my forehead, and I can feel his gentle claws in my hair like a metal spider. He begins to peck at the sausage roll. Hot flakes of pastry flitter down my face to my lap.

More jackdaws enter the confession box with their clacks and caws. To watch the procedure. I can feel the jackdaw's beak pierce the sausage meat and knock at my head. He knows what he is doing. Any pain I feel is drowned out by the excitement of being cleansed.

I close my eyes and let him pierce my skull, to tear the little pages from my head where my sins are written.

And he will drop them in a ditch for the weasels to read with their teeth.

The Cat Piss Astronaut

You'd been asking your mother to read the big encyclopedias to you. Even though she says that these are not the books that are supposed to be read to small children, these are the books for mammies and daddies to read. She says it in her high-pitched voice. But you tell her that your big brother said that the encyclopedias have all the big answers about the planets in the sky. You need the big answers and not the small answers. So she reads them to you. You get a flutter in your soul when you hear about the likes of Jupiter. A big spinning fella made out of hard gas with a surface that would turn you into a pebble if you put your feet on it. You paint Jupiter and Mars and Neptune on your blank pages with crayons and the paint that comes from the washing-up liquid bottles.

Your da asks why you won't sit still and have your bacon and cabbage. It will grow hairs on your chest, he says. You've checked your chest for hairs after eating bacon and cabbage before and none ever grow. There must be something wrong with you. You can't tell him the answer he wants to hear about the reason you won't eat.

Your mother gives in and makes you burgers and chips. It's your favourite meal. But what use is burgers and chips? You're not hungry, you need to think about Jupiter.

In school they tell you to stop flapping your hands and pacing when you talk about Jupiter. The teacher does sudden shouts at you.

'Sit down at your desk and shut up.'

'Why can't you do as you're told?'

When she says this, she ruins Jupiter. So the planet has to live only in your head again for a while.

You first start to become aware that you exist at about the age of five. You become aware that there's this shimmering confusion called reality, and you can't remember where you were before reality began. On Jupiter, there's reality too, but nothing like the reality here.

You memorise the planets in the solar system by their distance to the Sun. My Vest Eats My Jumper So Useless New Pullover.

Your mother reads the encyclopedia to you at bedtime and says that Jupiter is full of ammonia. You ask your mother what ammonia is. She gets annoyed and says that it's the smell of tomcats' piss.

The reality on Jupiter is so harsh that you're not even allowed to experience it. The blood in your veins would boil. Your head would pop, and your brains would turn to pasta in a wind made out of cats' piss that you can't hear, because nature made your ears to hear sounds in oxygen, not in the windy piss of cats. Your bones would be crushed. You find that funny. It makes the reality on Earth seem less serious. But you're glad that you live in the reality on Earth and not the reality on Jupiter where the wind is made of smelly tomcats' piss. You ask if you're allowed to have the light on tonight.

In school, your teacher asks you to step outside of the classroom. You hear the unsupervised laughter behind you because she leaves the door half open.

'Follow me quietly,' she says.

You both walk down the tiled corridor that has the big white statue of the man who is crying with his hands nailed. He is scary because adults don't cry. He is bigger than any adult you know. He stands at the end of the corridor. You always run past that statue when you need to go to the toilet. Even though you're not allowed to run in the corridor. Some days, you hold your pee in instead. You decided, the first time you saw the statue, that you would never ever ever look up at him again. People are very frightening when they are as still as the man with the nails in his hands. You've never met an adult or a child who could hold themselves that still before. The air around him smells like the smell from the back of your television at home. You think about his frozen marble face when you close your eyes at night time and you wish your mother would still let you sleep in her bed. But you're too old for that. It's not normal, she said.

This thought has made you walk slower, and you are flapping your fingers again and your head is somewhere different to the corridor. White sun is coming through the glass ceiling of the corridor that feels like when you put your face over the toaster to watch the bread turn into toast.

'Walk this way,' your teacher says to you, and she is louder now.

Her left hand swings faster than her right hand. Her hip moves to one side, sometimes she does coughs. You follow your teacher further down the tunnel.

Each cough from her is the exact same as the one before it and she brings her fist up to her mouth when it happens. You copy all of this behind her because she just told you to walk this way.

'Behave yourself,' she says, when you do coughs like her.

'You should be proud of this,' she says.

You don't know what that means, and you don't know why she has asked you to follow her or where you are going. When you get to the statue of the crying man, you really don't want to walk past him. Your heart is beating in a way that feels like it is in your neck. You are worried that your heart will fall out of your mouth on to the floor and that a dog will run away with it. You want to drink some water. The tears are burny behind your eyes and your forehead is like the nettles in the garden. You've been told that you are too old for crying, even though crying feels nice.

'I'm afraid of him and I don't want to walk underneath him,' you say.

'He loves you, he died for you,' she says. 'Come on, this way.'

You think about how you didn't ask the man to die, and it feels like you have killed him but can't remember when. You close your eyes so hard that the darkness becomes white and full of stars. This reminds you of Jupiter and you feel safe when you think of it. You use your ears to follow the sound of her steps and walk past the statue of the man with the nails in his hands and the frozen eyes. When you open your eyes, you don't know where you are any more.

Your teacher leads you into a new classroom that smells like varnish, and inside the new classroom is a new teacher who you've never seen before. A man teacher with metal hair like your father's, who smiles in a way that feels safer than the way your teacher smiles.

They both lead you to the top part of the class where you're not allowed to go unless you're asked to go there. You can see the teacher's desk up close. It has grown-up looking papers and a big chair. You stand underneath the blackboard. The class is full of older children, they look nine or even ten years old. They have pencils on their desks and not crayons. There are drawings and images of planets and the solar system all over the walls of their classroom. Turquoise Neptune, orangey Mars with the surface powdery like your da's snuff. A gigantic map of the Milky Way with all the foamy purples and whites. You cannot believe that the older children are doing planets for school when your class are only doing numbers from one to ten. Usually, you would start to cry if everybody stared directly at you like this. You don't mind the staring this time because the pictures of the planets make you feel incredibly happy and flappy.

Your teacher mentions your name. She is using the voice where she is both talking to you and talking to everybody at the same time. You've memorised this voice because it's a voice you only ever hear teachers use at school.

'Mr Cadogan is going to ask you some questions and we'd like you to answer to the class.'

The man, who must be Mr Cadogan, holds up a drawing of Jupiter.

'What is this planet?' he asks. His voice is kind.

'That's Jupiter,' you say.

He speaks your name in a soft way and asks, 'Will you please tell the class everything that you love about Jupiter?'

You immediately turn to all the bigger children. You feel intense joy and your fingers and feet are doing the things they do when you imagine Jupiter. The older children don't feel like faces of people now, they feel like a big blank page for you to paint. You say that Jupiter is the largest planet in our solar system. It's a gas giant, primarily composed of hydrogen and helium, similar to the Sun. Jupiter has a very strong magnetic field and the largest magnetosphere in the solar system. The planet is known for its Great Red Spot, a storm that has been ongoing for at least 300 years. Jupiter has 79 known moons – the four largest being Ganymede, Io, Europa and Callisto. Ganymede, Jupiter's largest moon, is even bigger than the planet Mercury. The planet has a faint ring system, composed of tiny dust particles. Jupiter's day is only about 9.9 Earth hours long, the shortest of all the planets. Jupiter's strong gravitational influence has been used to slingshot spacecraft on their long journeys. Jupiter is visible from Earth with the naked eye and was known to ancient astronomers. The wind is made from the piss of cats, and we would all die if . . .

'Thank you,' says Mr Cadogan.

Your teacher does the face. Some children have their mouths open and others are laughing, but Mr Cadogan starts clapping. And then all of the children start clapping because he is clapping. You start clapping too because everybody is clapping, and this is the first time that you ever liked anything that happened in school.

Mr Cadogan stops speaking in a way that is kind and then he is being loud and talking to his class and he says, 'He is only five years old, and he knows more about the planets than all of ye put together. And Mrs Flaherty here hasn't even taught his class about planets. They're in junior infants. He learned all of this himself. If a five-year-old can stand up at the top of this class and make fools out of you like this, then you all really need to pull up your socks.'

The older children look sad or angry or something in the middle of sad and angry. None of them even touch their socks. Everything about being alive feels frightening. Like you have done a bad thing by liking Jupiter so much.

Back home you can't sleep with the light off again. Your da says that you are too old to sleep with the light on. He puts glow-in-the-dark stickers of stars on the ceiling, but they don't look like real stars, they are stars for babies. He says the stars absorb sunlight in the daytime and emit it at night time when they glow. So it is real starlight on the ceiling, starlight that waits all day for you to sleep with the light off. This makes it okay. You've stopped asking your mother, what would my jacket look like if the wind was made of tomcats' piss that travelled at several hundred miles per hour? Why do I need to breathe? Does the oxygen make my blood move? So when I breathe out, the carbon dioxide goes from my lungs into that nettle over there? But then, that nettle breathes out oxygen at me? And I breathe that in, and it makes my blood move inside my body? Can I breathe the oxygen directly off a nettle? Why do nettles want to sting me? And what is breathing like on Jupiter, where there's helium and cats' piss wind instead of oxygen? Helium travels faster than oxygen, so would my blood move faster, would my life be shorter, because I'd be breathing a faster gas? What sound would the wind under the kitchen door make if it was helium? What would a nettle look like, if instead of carbon dioxide, it breathed in a wind of cats' piss, and then breathed out oxygen? What would my da's chest look like if it breathed out cat piss wind to feed the nettles? Would a nettle on Jupiter be green? Would it matter if it stung me when my body was exploding from the pressure? If I chose to stop breathing, would the nettles in the garden die?

When you flap your hands and pull your hair and pace around the kitchen, your mother asks you why you are so upset, and will you please stop doing these things, but you know that flapping and pacing are the best ways to visit Jupiter and feel safe.

★

When you are six, your older brothers and your ma and da run out of answers, and they don't have time to read the encyclopedias to you. They tell you that you are exhausting and that you should just look at the encyclopedias yourself. You don't know how to read them at first. You pick them by the letters. Your favourite is P, because the planets are in there. When the need for answers is so important, the words come to you. You figure it out yourself. A pattern emerges and you can trace its smell with your mind nostrils. Bits of words become the smell of a tomcat in your garage. Full stops are paw prints. Sentences have a song in them that you can learn like a tune.

You can read now. You can read better than every-body else in your classroom. Your mother, and your brothers tell you that you are brilliant. You've been eating encyclopedias. You are good. Instead of flap-ping and pacing you've started to keep your hands by your side, still like the statue in the corridor, and you curl your toes inside your shoes. It doesn't feel the same but other people are happier that way.

Your head is full of planets as you move towards the playground. The sky is the same colour as the long fluorescent lightbulb on the kitchen ceiling. When you were five, you would never go to the playground without your mother. That would have felt like dying. Even though the playground is right in front of your house, and you can see it from your bedroom window. Except in the night time, when you won't look out at the playground in case the statue man with the nails in his hands is there.

But now you are six, and all summer, you and your mother had practised being on your own in the playground. She would stand a little bit further back each day and wave at you when you look up from the swing. In her blue coat. The blue coat would be smaller every time. Until eventually, it became a tiny blue dot, and this felt okay because that's what the Earth would look like if you saw it from Jupiter. Then, on the last days of the practice, she just hung her coat on the front door of your house and went inside. Little blue Earth in the distance and you were on your own in the playground.

Now your mother doesn't even have to hang her blue coat on the door any more because you like being in the playground by yourself. You pull the zip up on your jacket because the playground is on the hill and is colder and the breeze travels down your neck. It feels good to do this for yourself. Your winter boots have brown-coloured fur inside and it feels thrilling to curl your toes back and forth.

There are two people in the playground today. A grown-up woman. She is wearing a blue coat just like your mother's. Except it is bigger and warmer looking than your mother's coat because of the winter. She is pushing a small girl on a swing. The girl must be her daughter. They are both laughing, and the girl does happy-sounding screams when she goes high up on the swing. It feels fun and safe when you watch them doing this. It doesn't feel like Jupiter, but it feels like when you think about Jupiter. This thought makes you think about Jupiter. The daughter is the same age as you, but you prefer talking to adults or older children because they know what planets are. Like when Mr Cadogan asked you to speak to the classroom last year and it was the only time you ever liked anything that happened in school.

You tell the woman that Jupiter is several times larger than the earth with a wind made from the piss of cats. Her face has a new way of squinting that you haven't seen before. She pushes her daughter on the swing more slowly now. The swing stops and the girl gets off. The girl looks at you but doesn't talk to you, instead she looks up at her mother. Her mother looks back at her, like she is talking to her daughter using only her face. You've seen your parents do this to each other before, but you don't know what it is and don't know how to ask what it is or why they do it. The woman and the daughter move away from where you are. They walk towards the slide.

You follow the woman, to tell her that if this playground existed on Jupiter, the helium in the air would make the swing move several hundred times faster. This would then propel her daughter into the air, and she'd be torn apart by a metallic cat piss wind and crushed to the size of a pebble by the gravity. But there is no need to worry because we are on Earth. And the swing set has been designed to accommodate our gravity, and our atmosphere. The woman does a smile when she hears this. It's the same smile your teacher did last year when you said 'fuck' out loud. The woman says, 'Aren't you very clever? Where is your mother at all?'

She asks your name, and you tell her that you are the Cat Piss Astronaut. She doesn't like this answer. It makes her do a quick breathing-in noise and she looks towards her daughter who wasn't even paying attention anyway.

They walk away from you, towards the nettles at the

edge of the playground, where the tarmac path is. But you follow them both so you can paint their blank pages with planets. You talk to the girl who is the same age as you. You tell her that we are very lucky to live on Earth, where everything in our reality is fine-tuned to the laws of this reality. Our jackets, our knees, the blood in our brains, the relationship between our breathing and the nettles that grow on the edges of the playground.

The more words you say, the faster the girl walks away from you. You don't understand why she and her mother aren't clapping. This feels frightening. You want to flap your hands, but that isn't allowed, so you stuff them hard into your pockets.

'Everything works together like the inside of an alarm clock,' you continue to say to the daughter as you follow her. 'Reality here on Earth, in this playground, is safe. Except in five billion years when the Sun will expand and our Earth will become like Jupiter. Then everything will end. There won't be any more reality. We will all explode.'

The girl isn't happy now and says that she would like to go home.

She asks, 'Mummy, will the Sun expand?'

Her mother says no. The mother tells her that you

are lying and are just making these things up to frighten her. She isn't talking like a grown-up any more. She is worried and angry at the same time and is talking to you like she is also a child.

'Why are you trying to frighten me? Tell us that you are lying,' she says. 'Tell us now that you are making this all up.'

You are not making this up. You feel very angry. Because you read in the encyclopedias that the Sun is a star, the same as any other star, and that stars expand, and when stars expand, they consume all the planets around them. Our Sun is no exception. There will be an end to all of this. Reality will die. This is a fact. You say all of this out loud at the woman and her daughter.

There is a sharp and shocking pain in your head. You feel like your brains are exploding – you think that you are on Jupiter. Your eyes are looking up towards the sky, but you didn't do this, something else is making you look at the sky. The woman with the blue coat like your mother's is pulling your hair. She is doing it as hard as she can. She is pulling your hair and making you walk away from her daughter. You can only see in front of you because she controls how you move your head with her hand. You can hear that her teeth are closed tight when she is talking. She is calling you a 'little knacker' and a 'gurrier'. She says 'shit' and 'fucking bastard' in a way that's quiet, like she wants to shout it really loud, but won't because those are adult words and her daughter is only six and might hear them. You are only six too.

You forget how to make sounds with your mouth and you truly believe that you are going to be killed by the woman and that this is the end of your life. You don't want to die because you love your mother and your father and your brothers, and you want more than anything in the entire world to be with them right now in your living room where it is warm and smells like dinners.

Your ears whistle like they are listening to a cat piss Jupiter wind, because she is hitting the top part of your head with her fist. You've never felt anything hit your head that hard before. Your scalp notices that she is wearing a metal ring and this spot is where all the pain comes from. Your face is very warm. She throws you on the concrete of the playground like a teddy bear. This has ripped the bit of your trousers where your knee is, and you can see your skin peeled back and it is all red. One of your boots with the brown fur is on the other side of the playground. You forget where the words are stored in your head.

The woman leaves the playground with her daughter. She is pushing her daughter because the daughter isn't running away fast enough. You look up towards your house and wish you could see the blue Earth of your mother's coat.

You run towards your house at a speed you didn't think you could achieve – it gets bigger, and time doesn't exist. You are pulled in by the gravity of it. You are burning up. You feel a deep, painful sadness because you've lost one of the new winter boots that your mother picked out for you, and this thought is the reason you start to cry.

You had eaten the encyclopedia.

You had found your own answers to the questions.

You thought you had been good.

When you tell your mother what happened in the playground, she asks you what you said to make the woman that angry.

The Poitín Maker

The ochre kernels of barley sifted through his calloused fingers, scarred from seasonal blisters. The grains had been soaking in the bloated bags for two days and two nights, woken by the silver water of the river. The sturdy odour of cereal hung in the earth of the hut. Tiny translucent hairs were sprouting from the base of each kernel. They looked like worms the way they pushed off the slimy husk of the seed. There must have been ten thousand of them in his four sacks. He picked one kernel and held it between his index finger and thumb in a pincer. As he squeezed it, he fixed a squint on the white paste that emerged from the bran. It stuck to his skin. He rubbed it between the tips of his fingers and pinched at the gummy resistance of it. There was a chalkiness that he felt in his back teeth. It was the malt. Pure starch. He thought about semen. His head flew off to an endless yellow field of barley with tall fronds tickling a low sun. The sadness and the fear entered him again because each one of these little sprouting barleys was a young life that he was cutting short.

He wiped his palms clean on the front of his trousers and stepped back from the sack of malting grains. The tightness was in his chest and travelled up to his forehead and furrowed a frown that was painful. It had the bones of a headache in it. Cait was bent over on the black floor of the hut. Her little chubby hands were playing in the dirt. She was forming balls of mud and squeezing them through her fingers. She smiled when she squeezed, and then the smile faded into the soft blankness of a daydream as her eyes focussed on the strings of mud that pushed through the gaps in her fist. It was a wonder and a curiosity, as if she was only now realising that she had that power in her hands.

He stooped down in a squat and put both his hands under Cait's oxters, then stood up and brought her chest close to his chest. She produced a gentle whisper of a gasp and whenever he'd hear it, he'd think about how small her lungs must be. He repositioned her so that her bum rested on the crook of his left forearm, his right palm supported her spine, and her head was nestled perfectly under his nose. As he bent low to walk out of the hut, he took deep breaths in through his nostrils, revelling in the smell of her hair and her scalp. It was like gorse flower or fresh milk or a strawberry. And it trickled down into the pit of his belly and flowed around his lungs. It tingled to the edges of his toes. It shone on any bit of anxiety in his body and cleansed the feeling with terrifying love. The sad pain in his forehead subsided and moved behind his eyes in a soothing balm. Tears formed. The healing tears that he'd search for whenever he smelled his daughter's hair.

Cait's left hand reached up towards the curls of his beard, just under his chin. She fondled and pulled like she'd find something in there. She was wiping off the mud from her palm. It hurt him a little. He pressed his neck closer to her fingers. She could clean her hands on his beard all day if she liked. The air cooled the tear on his cheek and they both gazed at the rolling bubbles of the stream. It was more of a river, but still a stream, somewhere in between. The ripples slushed over pebbles into deeper pools of dark water. The surface reflected the sky. He watched slender brown trout reposition themselves in unison. Blending into clouds of sand. They darted with the current so that he could only see them when he focussed intently. He blinked and he lost them. He found them again.

Blue mountains rose in the distance, watching him through the hazel trees on the other side of the stream. The mud hut was to his back, like the den of an animal. He had built it in this spot three autumns ago by piling dense, grey sods of river-bed clay between layers of willow branches, eventually forming a wall. The exact spot was chosen with incredible care. A small, leafy ravine that looked like the earth had been split open with a hatchet long ago. Hidden away from eyes. The water too shallow for any person to pass by on an oar boat. The hut leaned into the crevice of a limestone rock face that was just tall enough to dissipate the white smoke from his still. The roof had a chimney hole and was thatched with fresh lumps of grass and ferns as green as the natural thickets that grew around them. If any passing person was ever to look down into the ravine, they'd have to focus intently to see the hut. But no person would ever find him. He knew that.

A dusk breeze came down the water and Cait did her gasp again. The creeping chill of late autumn. He hoisted her up closer to his elbow so that her chest was nearer the warmth of his body, steadying her again with his palm. Her middle was sturdy and she could support her neck. She was almost as heavy as a bag of dry barley but nowhere near as heavy as a bag of wet barley. The sun hid over the limestone ravine and cast a shadow. Everything became dull as the air cooled. A cormorant landed on a rock a slight distance upstream. It was a silhouette in the fading light. It spread its two black velvety wings wide, shaking them in a slow dance, its serpent neck tapering up into a sharp beak. Cait jolted in his arms with excitement and pointed at the bird. 'Gack, gack,' she said. Her eyebrows raised as if they were ready to jump off her forehead. A look of new surprise and amazement took over her face. 'Gack, gack,' pointing more at the cormorant, like she could reach over and touch it. The terror and tightness returned to his chest. He felt that they were being monitored. He quickly turned his shoulders to the water, retreating inside the hut with Cait firmly in his arms. She squirmed to look back at the bird.

The poitín hut was smaller than their stone cottage over the hill, but there was enough space for him to stand upright in the centre. The mud walls made the whole place smell like being buried alive. It was very dark. A turf firepit in the centre gave off a faint orange glow about as bright as two candles. He sat Cait on a bed of straw and fed her a gluey meal of barley porridge and smoke-dried trout in a wooden bowl. The bowl rested in between her thighs. She ate with her hands, and her little face took on a studious look when she savoured the food. He tipped water against her lips from his tin cup and her fingers stained the sides with gruel. He basked in her delight. A pride filled his belly when he recognised that something he had prepared could bring her such pleasure and vitality. She paused between bites and looked at him with an urgency. 'Gack, gack,' she'd say in an excited pitch. He smiled back at her, saying yes yes. Not understanding what she was trying to say, but truly believing that it was very important to her, whatever it was. He didn't eat.

Pitch darkness came outside and he knew she'd be getting tired and cranky soon. He set to work on the soaked barley. He had crocheted a robust drying rack, woven in a teepee shape from bendy branches of blackened willow that had been smoke hardened over the years. It could hold significant weight despite its spindly appearance. It was taller than him and was situated over the glowing embers of peat turf. It reached up so that the top was just under the chimney hole in the roof.

He settled a barley sack on the bottom tier of the rack which was interlaced in a hatched pattern. Using his knife, he cut a careful slit down the centre of the coarse bag. He pulled the hessian apart. All the barley swooshed in a triangle pile on the splayed sack. The white sprouts of each grain caught the glowing light in the dark and stared up at him like red eyes in a forest. This made him pause for a bit. Cait was playing with her empty wooden bowl behind him and making little groans of frustration. A few kernels rolled towards her, and she crawled forward with a curious hand unfurled. He swept them away with his palm before she could put them in her mouth. He quickly got back to work. Spreading the barley out evenly on the fabric with his palms. He repeated this four times on each shelf of the drying rack, so the gentle heat of the peat fire could rise up through the striating layers of grain and draw the moisture out. This would stop the seeds from germinating and complete the malting process. It would take all night to do this.

He arranged straw on the bare mud floor beside the rack. On a strip of hessian he placed a smoked trout and a small tin cup of water. Next to this were several sods of fresh turf and a set of iron tongs. The turf was well dried and he dug it himself from the bog of skulls at the feet of the blue mountains. It would produce hardly any smoke, nor would it impart too strong a peat taste on the barley malt. He sat down with his shoulders against the natural limestone wall at the back of the hut. It was cold but his feet reached the rim of the fire. He rehearsed picking up a piece of turf with the tongs and dropping it in the fire, making sure his arm had enough of a span to do this without needing to get up from where he lay. When he was satisfied that everything was in its place, he called to Cait. She was rubbing her eye with her fist. He said, 'Night, night,' and she understood this and crawled towards him as best she could. He reached out and laid her whole body on his chest. He relished the warmth of her back. She slumped into him, her head under his chin and her feet reaching down to the top of his thighs. He wrapped Cait in her red blanket made from wool. Tight and cozy, up to the top of her belly so that she could still move her arms. She looked up towards the chimney hole where the smoke escaped. His lips pressed against the back of her head and he noticed the warming fog of his own breath. He admired the perfect softness of the left side of her face. His two hands secured her in place. She began to wail. She reached behind her head and tugged at the curls that finished on the back of her neck. She pulled at the hairs of his beard. He knew this meant that she was very tired and needed help falling asleep.

When Cait would cry in the hut, a great panic would consume him. He worried that she might feel his heart pounding against her back and then bawl through the night. He told himself that the thick mud sods in the walls would dampen the sound of her cries. He told himself that the rushing of the stream outside would overpower the noise she made. He could deal with a human hearing her. But dusk was when the fairies listened out for babies. He inhaled the perfume of her scalp through his nostrils. His heart lulled in his chest. He rocked his torso and sang a whispered lullaby until her wailing became a quieter, rhythmic groan that matched the tempo of his movement. When she drifted off, he placed the warm iron tongs between his hand and her chest. To protect from the fairies' magic and to help transport Cait into a deep sleep. He listened to the pace of her breath, scrunching the muscles around his eyes to hone in on the sound. There was always a ringing in his ears. Like distant bells. He couldn't remember how long he'd lived with the bells in his head. He'd only noticed them when Cait was a few weeks old and a tiny breath was something he needed to hear.

As the air from her nose flowed heavy and slow, he cautiously took the iron tongs from her chest and placed a fresh sod of turf on the embers. He watched the orange glow creep and singe the fibres. Clean heat wobbled the air like worn glass and distorted the yellow barley. He wondered if she was old enough to have dreams yet. The sound of water rippled outside. When Cait slept, he had the misfortune of being alone with his thoughts. How the fairies had taken her brother in the night and replaced him with a changeling. They come for the baby boys. Intrusive images nailed themselves to his head. The month-old baby stiff in his straw cot on that morning. A frozen face like a little apple made out of candle wax. No priest would bless the dead child. You can't bury a changeling in a graveyard. His two hands thatching his son's body into the roof of the cottage, with an iron horseshoe for protection. Was it his son in the ceiling or the fairy child they left in his place? The fairies had taken Cait's mother too. In a fever the week after Cait was born. In the daytime he kept his hands busy to stop himself from thinking about his wife and his son. He couldn't even say their names. And he knew with utter certainty that it was all his fault. He had been targeted by the fairies because of what he did with the barley and the still. Every drop of spirit stolen from a grain belongs to the Otherworld. They'll take their reparations. He was haunted by the sound of them coming for Cait, in the tiny bells that they put in his head.

Cait was born a boy, but he's raising her as a girl. He'll grow her hair out long and put her in dresses when she's older. All to trick the fairies. And that stayed locked in his mind with the visions of her dead mother and brother. She was Cait, she was nothing other than Cait. But he knew that cormorant had its eye on her when it did the dance on the stream. That was no cormorant. His heart got loud again and the chilled sweat bloomed out of the pores of his forehead. He felt the powerful urge to get up and walk it off. Cait blubbered an irritated groan and exhaled, as if her body sensed his intentions. She was a ball of heat on his chest. He moved his left hand up slightly so that it rested under hers. Her hot palm gripped his finger from the depths of her sleep and he was frightened by how much he loved her. The barley made crackling noises. He dipped his other hand in the tin cup and flicked water on the burning turf. It hissed and white smoke swirled up and out the roof. He hoped that it wasn't seen in the sky.

The song of a thrush brightened the ravine. Perfect beams of blue light penetrated every fault in the mud and shone through the smoke of the hut. Cait awoke with a groggy cry. She had relieved herself in her sleep.

He cleaned her off and quickly washed his soiled shirt in the stream. Beside him, she swept at grass with her hands and tried to place some in her mouth. Wisps of dawn fog curled over the surface of the water. He focussed on them from his knees, and in that small moment he was not consumed by worry or guilt. He moved her to his lap. They ate porridge and butter-milk warmed in the ash of the sods.

The barley kernels were bone dry from the night. The malt was complete. He sniffed them in his palm. The sweetness of cereal climbed up the hairs of his nostrils and finished with the smoggy violence of peat. His thoughts could taste their spirits in the arse of his throat. They would make a fine poitín.

Cait's blanket was stretched over the grass by the edge of the stream. She had only learned to crawl a month ago, but stayed within the warmth of the wool-len surface. He settled two oak barrels in front of the hut, aged and coopered with rusted iron bands. They'd been buried near by when he did this last year. All his equipment was hidden and buried near the ravine, with the exception of the copper worm. He arranged the barrels so that he could see Cait while he worked. Their rims reached his thighs. He emptied the malted barley into both of the barrels. White powder kicked up from the starch of the grain and chalked his beard. Squatting with a stable back, he lugged a tin milk-churn on to a three-legged grate and set it there. He lowered a tanned ceramic jug into the stream with both hands and slooshed it into the churn until it was full of water. A fire of turf and sticks was lit under the base. Flames blackened the bottom. The stream carried a breeze that flumed the smoke into the hazel trees. The leaves ate the plumes. They didn't slither above the ravine. Cait played with her bowl and paused when damp wood popped in the fire. 'It's okay,' he said to her.

As he waited for the water to boil, a white butterfly jittered over the grass. It landed on the red fabric of Cait's woollen blanket, confusing it for a flower. Slow movements. Fanning its wings with a delicate grace that caught the sunlight and glinted. Cait reached for the butterfly. 'Gack,' she said. She planted her palm down on its body and pressed it against the wool. Her face with the daydream gaze. He looked up from the bubbles of the heating churn and screamed at her. 'No.' She recoiled and began to cry. He had never shouted at her like that before. It was the same guttural cry she made the time she accidentally burned her hand on a kettle. He rushed to her side and picked her up. Rocking her and kissing her forehead. Her face was pink and swollen with tears as she wailed through the ravine. Birds flew from a hazel. Spit dripped from her mouth and her few small teeth were visible. 'I'm sorry. Shhh, shhh,' he said. 'I'm so sorry.' Her crying faded into staggered anxious gasps which were somehow more painful to him than bawls. He rubbed his cheek against her tears and wished that he could put them back into her eyes. They were diamonds to him. The morning had been peaceful and now he had ruined it. He hated this world where she experienced hurt and terror. He despised himself for being the source of it. The butterfly was still alive. He peered down and watched it unfold its snowy wings against the scarlet blanket. Cait's hand on the soft wool had not been powerful enough to injure it. After a few seconds it fluttered off again over the stream. He held Cait close in his two arms. He told himself that it was just a white butterfly. Even though he knew what they said about white butterflies. But it was definitely just a harmless butterfly. He tried desperately not to entertain the fear that the butterfly was the soul of her dead brother who had come from the fairy world to warn them. Steam puffed from the boiling water of the churn. He wanted to hold her to his body all day but the job wouldn't wait.

He took a baton to the malted grains that rested in the wooden barrels and crushed them under the cudgel. Beating the wood like a drum. He sung the song his mother sang when he'd watched her do the same. The chaff separated under the battering until a coarse raggedy yellow meal remained. He poured boiling water from the churn and scalded it. He did this until the barrels were almost full and the oak was warm to the touch. The kernels floated up and frothed at the surface, releasing the stodge from their endosperms. With two fists around the long wooden baton, he stirred the mixture anticlockwise in a gentle vortex. The swirling grains were hypnotic and they released him from his ever-present sensation of panic. Plumes of steam sweated up the hairs of his forearms and condensed in dripping beads on his face. The mixture resembled the grey porridge that they ate. The barley bloomed in the scald and the dead grains diffused their full bouquet. His seasoned nose took in hazelnuts rolled in burning sugar, goats' cream about to sour, a new turned sod of earth on bruised grass, stained with the dungy viscera of a lamb's birth, the stolen nectar of a foxglove, toasted bread, the screams of a widow after a battle, a thousand yards of peat bog under thunder and the sharp zest of vomit. Every seed was a unique life with a story and an ancestry and he had no business translating these ghosts into a bottle for a human to comprehend with their lips. He released heavy black treacle from a ceramic pot and it folded on the meniscus and sunk below the liquid to the bottom of the barrels. He agitated the grey wash and the sweetener stained it sienna. From his waistcoat pocket he produced the yeast wrapped in butter paper. A live culture that might be three hundred years old and passed down from distiller to distiller. Yellow and doughy with a sickly essence. It would devour the barley starch and treacle to excrete them as heady alcohol. He scraped the yeast into the barrels and covered them with their lids, leaving enough space at the top for the bubbles of the wash to burp. He draped the wood in an olive-drab wax tarp that could stand a bit of rain if it came. He would leave it now for a week until it awoke for the still.

He wrapped Cait to his chest, with their few important belongings in a sack on his back. Performing the necessary precautions of subterfuge around the hut before they left. The olive tarp of the barrels was staggered with some ferns to break up their shape. The milk churn and any other instruments were placed back in the hut with the opening shut. From her bundle on his midriff, Cait reached out helpful hands at every object he grabbed and said 'Gack' and squealed. Any trace of a firepit near the stream was dug up with the heel of his boot and covered in grass. They exited the ravine by the end of the stream where it tapered off into a wider river. Up the slant of a mossy hill and through the heather of the moor until they found the grey-shaled bóithrín. The blue mountains stood watch like impartial deities. He began the trek back to their cottage.

It was midday and Cait was stirring in the bundle under his chin. There was nothing strange about a man and his daughter travelling home on the moor. He stood taller on the path than he had done in the ravine. One arm swung and the other supported Cait's back. The odd bit of sun warmed the top of his head. They passed a raggedy tent on wooden poles with a look of the fabric of the barley sack about it. He couldn't tell if the people inside had no belongings or if they were transient. A man lay at the entrance in a stupor with his face pointing up at the sky, drunk as drunk could be. His body had sunk into the mud like the earth had no teeth and was slowly sucking him down with sloppy brown gums. A bare-chested child of about five wore a loincloth and was playing with a grey dog who bounced and barked. The child barked back at the dog and was indifferent to its father in the mud. He slowed his step until he wasn't moving. His shoulder pointed towards the tent with a tension of intent in his tilted neck, like he would stop to check on the man and the child. The ground off the path was marshy. He kept walking on and wondered if he had distilled the bottle that caused all of this.

Cait always slept easy when his silent body produced heat and rocked her with the predictable rhythm of his pace. It was clear heather moors for acres on either side of the crumbling path. The shadow of a cloud dragged across the side of a mountain in the distance and disappeared. The rock face lit up bright purple with the flowers of the heather. A fox emerged from a trail ahead of him, bushy tailed. It stopped in the centre of the road, looked at him and Cait, then moved to the other side and was gone. It was definitely just a fox. The animals didn't frighten him out here in the open.

Cait was waking in the bundle when he came up the hill to his cottage. She did cranky little groans that shook off her sleep. He moved closer to the cottage and noticed a single white sheet hanging on his washing line. A worry came over him. He had not put it there. It was a message from the gadger Mulqueen.

One white sheet on the line meant the gadger would need the stock of poitín in one week. There must have been a wedding suddenly announced down in the village, or maybe some person was at the door of death and there would be need of spirits at their wake. Whatever it was, the gadger had a sudden demand for drink, and it was none of his business who bought it and why. Sure he didn't sell it, he just made it for the gadger to sell. But a week was too soon. The malt was only put to ferment that morning. He'd have to rush the distillation and risk producing a spirit that could blind a person, or worse, kill them stone dead. If he refused, he'd be in debt to the gadger and his men. A rotten shower of thugs.

There was nothing special about their cottage, but it wasn't a tent on the side of the road either. Walls of stone with a limewash and a strong roof of thatch. It always stayed dry inside. The wood of the door was heavy and it could tell you stories about battles it had won with February winds. There was a pine table by the fire. Two chairs and a cotton mattress full of straw. A dresser that was taller than him. Cait had her own cot with high sides that enveloped her. And he could afford the rent of it, no fear of a bailiff around here. They had been away for a week and the stones in the wall had sucked in the cold. There were piles of wood adjacent the hearth of the fire. He lit them and the room filled up with warmth. Cait was wide-eyed and sat up on her blanket. She reached out her hand and pointed at the objects around the room like they were old friends: the wooden butter churn in the corner, the oil lamp on the table, and Cait's doll that sat on the top shelf of the wooden dresser. She was excited and he was glad that she was home in comfort and not in the cold of the mud hut.

The sky outside grew mauve. Cait fell asleep in his arms and he lay her down in her cot. He had prepared a quick dough for bread earlier; it rested in a blackened pot that was smothered in ashy coals. A smell of baking stuck to the air. The embers of the hearth glowed just enough that he could save the bit of oil in the lamp for another time. Cait's slumber was all consuming; she was surrounded by the familiar smell of her home. He placed an iron poker that had warmed near the fire across her chest to protect her from fairy magic in the night.

Quietly, he removed a bottle of whiskey from the dresser and sat down at the wooden table. He wiped away flour and dough with the edge of his palm. The crown stamp was torn under the cork. The stamp let him know that the necessary taxes had been paid and that this was a regulated and legal bottle of alcohol. He'd spent a fair bit on this bottle last year. He poured a small measure into a cup and topped it up a quarter way with water. The bottle went back in the dresser. The whiskey was the colour of strong tea. He lifted it under his nose and marvelled at the aroma of butter and bubbling sugar. The alcohol odour was pure with no fruity trace of the dreaded methanol. The sip he took was miserly. Just enough to dance around his mouth and burn his throat. He could make spirit as good as this if he had the equipment and the time to age it in the barrels, without fear of them being dug out of the bog by the revenue men. And it wasn't his fault either, that the safe stuff was beyond the means of the ordinary people of the countryside. He was only meeting a demand. If he didn't do it, someone else would. He inserted his index finger in a remnant of itinerant bread dough that rested on the wooden table. It was puffy and raw from the yeast. The dough sucked the tip of his finger down and smothered it in its beige sludge.

The harsh lick of winter was almost in the air. He watched Cait sleep and gulped the last of the cup of whiskey. He clenched his jaw in anger, grinding so hard that he felt the sugar in the drink between his back teeth. He thought about the money he'd earn from the gadger for a full delivery of poitín, and he inventoried the next eight months in his head. The rent paid to the landlord, six bags of flour, churns of milk, plenty of oats, coal, the few spuds in the ground outside the door. He could buy a young pig and fatten it come November, and himself and Cait would have salted bacon hung from the rafters until May. His eyes moved up to the rafter where he envisioned the hanging pig. To the right was the spot where he'd thatched his baby son's body into the straw of the roof. Tiny porcelain bones now he supposed, encircled by the iron protection of the horseshoe. Or maybe he was still there the way he found him that morning, because changelings don't rot? Little fleshy dolls made as a joke in the Otherworld from materials he can't even fathom. And what was the point in even thinking about it anyway, because he'd never dare check to find out. He saw the sour head on the priest who refused to bless the stiff little body in the cot. Did the priest actually refuse to bless the dead boy because it was a fairy child? Or was it a cruel human punishment for how the boy's father paid the rent? At least the fairies would never look down at you. If you took from them, they took something back, and that was that.

He moved his left foot to his heel and slid off the boot on the other foot. The leather made a squeaking sound against his skin. He reached down and took off the right boot with his hand. He got up from the wooden chair with his two hands on the table so that it didn't scrape against the stone floor. He crept over to Cait as she lay in the cot, negotiating with the smack of his bare soles on the stone. Cartilage of bone cracked in his knees and betrayed his attempt at silence. He bent and kissed her forehead, reassured by the heat of her skin on his lips. She had the look of her mother from this angle. He listened for the breath from her nose, but the bells in his head were too loud from thinking about the priest. When she gets old enough, maybe five or six, she'll start asking questions about whether she is a boy or a girl. He will deal with it then. It will be up to her then. The fairies will have moved on if they can just keep it going till then.

He let five days pass in the warmth and dryness of their cottage. His head was away in the rising bubbles of the barrels in the ravine. On the sixth day, the fizz of the ferment sang to him across the moors and called out for his intervention. From the rafter he took down the worm of the still and held it aloft in his fists like a curly sword. The worm was a winding brushed copper tube, a rose-orange tangle of metal that glimmered like the inside of an oyster shell around the bends of its coils. The open ends crusted turquoise in a verdigris rust. It had been hammered out by a rare craftsman of the ditch and then blessed by a fairy doctor in a holy well. The worm was the tunnel through which he saw life in the Otherworld and stole it. It was a pink-eyed, all-white badger and the collarbone of a saint. Not a hope would he risk stowing it in the mud poitín hut with the rest of his instruments. He circled the worm at his feet and stood back admiring it. Cait entertained herself on the floor with a strand of yellow straw, chewing it and relieving the soreness of her teething gums.

On the stone slabs, he rested the worm on a yard of cloth and wrapped the coils tenderly. In that brief moment there was something in front of his eyes that he worshipped as much as his daughter. Cait watched him coddle the copper worm with about as much patience as an infant could muster. He packed it with the straw and twine so that it looked like a square bale on his back. He then took Cait in his arms and secured her in the bundle under his chin. There was no space on his back, so he hung a compact lamb's leather pouch from Cait's waist, placing in this some bread, stewed apples, and cheese. But not so much that it would burden her.

From the threshold, his eyes scanned back over the room. He tapped an iron key off the wood of the door, and said to himself in a whisper, 'You've put out the fire. You've packed everything. You've put out the fire. You've packed everything.' He repeated this four times, and turned back in the threshold twice, to make sure that he had put out the fire and packed everything. Cait began to whimper and struggle in the bundle. She reached up towards her doll on the dresser. The doll was wooden and had a polished ceramic face. Its timber ribs were covered in a bright blue dress with a head of hair that had curls like hanging sausages. He was reluctant to bring it with them to the poitín hut in case it got damaged or dirty. He wasn't made of new dolls. But now that Cait had pointed at it, he couldn't risk her crying all the way back to the ravine and drawing attention to them. He handed her the doll, and she said 'Aaaaah' and hissed out smiles. Tugging at the doll's hair and soothing herself.

He locked the door of their home. They exited the cottage at dusk and cut across the field to the route that led to the ravine. He fed Cait morsels from his fingers as they moved. She ate lumps of cheese and stewed apple and fell asleep in the bundle with her legs dangling and rapping off his thighs. He retrieved the doll from the clutch of her sleeping hands and tucked it inside the leather pouch around her waist. An accusatory moon saucered up in the stars and it lit the wild path with a paleness that turned shapes into faces. It wasn't great for his imagination. The terror returned in the sweat under his arms. Slumbering Cait dragged down his chest. Crossing the moor, he stooped from the weight of the worm and the moonlight cut him a beastly side profile. The mountains and their heather were only a rumour in the blackness. He thought he saw a fairy light flicker up over the bogs and disappear again. He heard the crunch of the shale bóithrín under his feet. He listened to bats swoop over the midges that bit at the grease of his scalp. The tent with the drunk man and the barking child was gone or swallowed by mud. Catching sight of Cait's white breath in a lunar beam, he tasted the damp and chill in the air. The chatter of the stream was close. He held her two feet in his palms as they negotiated the hill down the ravine and entered the mud hut for the night. He didn't sleep and she did.

He set to work at the first glimmer of dawn. Cait ate porridge from the wooden bowl; it stuck to her fingers and got in her hair. He gently plucked the gloop from the strands before it dried and nestled her on her red blanket with the doll. Peeling off the drab tarp, he scored the knife tip under the lid of the first barrel and sensed a new pressure that was not there when he sealed it a week ago. With the weight of his wrist on the knife handle, he pried the wooden lid open and felt the pop. He watched vapour emerge against the trees in the foreground, and the barrel fizzed with enthusiasm. Bubbles rose up in the caramel liquid and frothed a yellow scum at the top that reminded him of an elderly malicious river. The piquant hammer of alcohol met his nose. He dipped a glass in the barrel and held it to the sky. The morning sun shot through the bubbles and cast an auburn stained-window shadow over his eye. He put it to his lips. The excited ghosts of barley kernels scarpered around the purgatory of his tongue and he spat them out on a dock leaf. He let the air of the bog enter his mouth and noted the uncorrupted fermentation of the brew.

On the grass by the stream, he blended coarse flour and water in a bowl and kneaded it into a fist-sized ball of dough. It was speckled and rough. He left it to breathe. He kept one eye on Cait and ran to pick her up when she crawled from her blanket. Flat rocks were lifted from the bed of the stream. He arranged them in two piles near the edge of the water, one taller than the other. The taller pile had a chamber in the middle; it was the firepit. Sods of turf and sticks were placed in the chamber. He walked towards the hut to quickly retrieve the components of the poitín still.

In the brightness of the sun, he detected footprints in the mud around the entrance of the hut. They were impressions of a cloven hoof like those of a goat. He sensed terrible burning fright in the pit of his stomach and it went up into his head where his thoughts were and began to control them in a very cruel way. What if they were the footsteps of a divil or púca who had come to find Cait while they had slept inside during the night? What if it was watching them now? What if it had made its mind up and there was nothing he could do to stop what was going to happen to her? He turned to look at Cait. She stared up at his eyes and stopped playing with the doll. He scanned the trees and the water for danger. They all blurred into one threatening visage. His breath was up in his throat and he felt like he was dying. He hoisted Cait up and tried to protect as much of her body with his arms as he could. A panicked right hand grasped at her shoulder and then clasped her two feet. It was cold. Cait's bottom lip quivered and her face became pink. His heart hammered at the bones of her chest. He considered abandoning the entire distillation process there and then. She cried. He kissed her forehead and the smell of her hair helped him to slow his breathing down. He listened to the air swoosh through the hazel trees. Down the ravine in the distance at the end of the stream he could now see a red deer fawn among the trunks of the trees. Beautiful and peaceful with a coat like flour flicked on a toasted loaf, its head grazing the earth. Calmer now, he traced the cloven footprints from the hut entrance with his eyeline and they led in the direction of the deer. With Cait hunkered against his ribs, he entered the hut and saw that the leftover piles of malted barley had been disturbed by an animal's muzzle. He felt relief and he felt foolish. He saw himself telling the gadger about confusing a little deer for the púca fairy and how he nearly didn't distil the poitín. And the coins in the gadger's hand and his dirty fingernails and his sneaky laugh. He situated Cait back down near the firepit outside the hut. She was still upset, but he didn't have the time to console her. He rapidly retrieved the milk churn, a copper kettle, a pipe, and a few dozen glass bottles that were stored in the hut.

He hauled the tin milk churn on to the flat rocks of the firepit. Using the big jug, he filled it with the fermented barley brew from the wooden barrels. It fizzed and small bubbles danced up over the brim of the churn. A copper kettle with a spout was secured on top of the churn. The burnished metal was cool against his skin. He had cut out the bottom of the kettle so that it had no base. It would be the head of the still where the vapours collect. He took pinches of the coarse dough from the bowl. At the seam where the kettle rested on the churn, he moulded the dough to create a seal. He smudged the putty with his thumb, pressing and kneading until no vapours would escape. Cait was crawling by his feet. She took twigs from the firepit and broke them in her hands and put them back. He was afraid she might knock a churn on top of her. He moved her. On the shorter of the rock piles, he rested a wooden barrel that had a hole at its base. The coiled copper worm was lowered into this barrel; it was a perfect fit. The worm spiralled, orange and metallic, from the top of the barrel to the bottom, and the end poked out of the hole in a spout. Watertight around the hole. A pipe connected the spout of the kettle to the top of the worm. Both ends sealed with the dough. He filled the barrel with very cold water from the stream. He peered down into the clear water and watched how the submerged coil was distorted in size under the surface.

He placed Cait on her blanket, which was a safe distance away from the still. A ball of dry straw nestled among the hazel twigs and turf sods of the firepit. He knapped lively sparks from his flint rock. They kindled the hay. Wisps of white smoke licked out like tongues and he blew on them. Flames came into being as if given permission from his breath. Everything crackled and popped. The turf began to burn with the tiny green flames he'd see over the bogs in darkness. The flickers reflected in his pupils and he felt the heat on his face. Angry orange fire rose up the base of the blackened churn and the doughy seals at the seams of the metal shrank and hardened like white plaster. It was still blue early morning.

He set a glass bottle directly under the worm spout at the base of the barrel. It would take at least twenty minutes before the fire started to heat the fermented wash in the still. He waited.

The blanket was comfortable under him, next to Cait. He stroked her arm. The calluses of his skin scraped off her skin and she recoiled instinctively. He experienced shame and guilt, and told her that it was just a deer earlier and that there was no need for her to be as upset as she was. He sat with his legs crossed and lifted Cait so that she rested on his thighs facing him. He held her hands and doted on her, telling her in high-pitched whispers how much he loved her. She looked back at him, her eyes wide and affectionate, a feathery smile with soft teeth. She stared directly into his face with an awesome glare of pure innocence and unconditional love, and when she did this he broke eye contact and felt deeply undeserving. A confusing flicker of resentment towards Cait glimmered in an untrodden part of his brain. And then he knew that he was a despicable person. The churn began to rumble with the boil inside.

He stalked around the side of the gurgling still. A pinhole of vapour hissed through a seam on the kettle. He thumbed dough over the orifice. The churn growled and staggered. He poured quenching water on the fire underneath to modulate the aggression of the distillation. Squeezing his palm around the pipe that connected the kettle and the copper worm, it felt blood-warm and pulsed with the chug of the spitting brew. Alcohol vapour coursed down the submerged coil and condensed into liquid when it hit cold copper. Poitín trickled out of the turquoise lip of the spout into the glass bottle. He splashed more water on the fire. Opaque smoke wafted through the ravine and stung his eyes. The spirit spurted out until it stopped about three-quarter ways up the glass bottle. He held it up to his eye. It was like water clouded with a thimble of milk. Under his nose, the odour attacked with an acridity that split a squirm through the middle of him and echoed back up his mouth in a gawk. He salivated. It retreated with the fruitiness of a withered brown apple. He shook a drop on the fire and it exploded in a green flame the way poitín doesn't. The ghost of the spirit was demonised by vitriol. He would not even taste this. It was methanol. The poisonous singlings of the grain that he expected from the first run of distillation. The singlings were the property of the fairies and could only be drunk by the fairies. He held the bottle in front of his chest with inertia, as if he was considering the tradition of throwing it over his left shoulder as an offering to them. There was no point. The fire picked up pace and he let the cloudy methanol fill the bottles.

The sun was higher in the sky now. He rapped the tin churn to hear its hollow clank. Eight bottles of milky fluid rested on the grass by the river, ready to be corked. The fire was only ashy coals. Cait was seated in his left arm and was groaning in the cranky way that implied hunger. Tears and commotion if he didn't feed her soon. After they ate a lunch, he would fill the churn up again with the wash from the barrels and begin another distillation. He'd repeat this until he had twenty-four bottles of poitín ready for the gadger that night.

On Cait's blanket they sat together. The water was at their feet with the mud hut behind them and the still to the left. Brown as the pebbles beneath, the trout were hidden in their forever dance with the current of the water. He watched spidery looking flies skirting across the deeper pools of the stream. Satisfying circles rippled out when a fish surfaced to bite. The ravine had a peace in the ether and the leaves of the hazel didn't sway at all. The bread he had baked was round like a mushroom. Tanned and blackened from the hearth. The crust made a tapping noise in his hands. His fingers pulled apart the loaf in two halves and revealed the spongy innards with big creamy holes of air. It smelled like the comfort of their cottage over the moor. He pinched at the soft bread and rolled it in a ball. He inserted some cheese and handed it to Cait.

She gummed at the morsel and clasped her hands, studying the food in her mouth with her serious expression. He smirked at her face in adoration. He ate too, and relished the tang and resistance of the toasted crust against his teeth. He'd made a pot of black tea on the firepit embers and drank it warm and tannic from the vessel it brewed in. The tea coaxed out the unctuousness of suet in the bread.

He was distracted by the eight bottles of poitín that stood on the grass in the corner of his eye. The pale greyness of their fluid brought up the shame in him. If he could only have a week to let them sit and then run it through the still a second or third time, he could purify it and make it safer to drink. Ideally a month to breathe in a barrel after. But even one more time through the still would nearly be enough to sort it. Maybe if he'd have thrown a few lumps of charcoal in a funnel under the spout, that might have extracted some of the badness before it went in the bottle. Why didn't he think of that? His feet stretched beyond the red blanket towards the mud of the stream bed. The heels of his boots indented in the sludge of the earth and sank a bit. He watched the mud envelop the leather. He knew the gadger Mulqueen wouldn't give two fucks about the colour of the drink. The gadger would have no bother on him watering it down and cutting it with horses' piss to hide the fruity tones of the methanol. It was none of his business what the gadger did or who bought the bottles. And it was the gadger and his bedsheet who told him to rush the whole thing anyway. He gritted his teeth again and evicted bread from a molar with his tongue.

Cait had eaten well, and was stroking her doll's dress and making cooing noises in a languid state of satiation. She sat up between his legs with her back to him, his left hand was on her left shoulder and his other hand was across her chest. He raised a finger and felt the softness of her ear and the wisps of her hair. He tried to bend his chest forward, to kiss the crown of her scalp, but her head was just beyond the reach of his lips. He watched the surface of the stream with intent and tried to locate the trout underneath. A quick shadow blackened a ripple and his eyes flew up. It was the cormorant flapping up above. The bird landed in a pool of the stream where the water was slower and deep, about two yards from him and Cait. It bobbed on the water with the look of a malnourished swan, much smaller than when its wings were outstretched. The slick iridescence of its plumage scintillated like black pearls you wouldn't see on a divil's necklace.

Feathers shifted shapes in front of him. The panic came up into his forehead, but he was determined not to react to this feeling after the incident with the deer. He focussed on its snakey head and the tiny scythe at the end of its beak. He couldn't decide if the bird was monitoring Cait or if that was just the way it held its head. Slowly, the cormorant arched its slender neck back, raising its beak skyward, and then sprang forward and disappeared its entire body under the water. It barely created a ripple. The eyebrows raised on his face as he waited for the diving cormorant to return to the surface. He was unable to tell if time was slowing down in the moment or if the cormorant was really under the water for that long. How could it stay down that long? It must have been two minutes. He became aware of his tongue in his mouth and the metallic taste of his saliva. He wondered if he controlled his tongue or if his tongue controlled itself and what was prevent-ing him from swallowing his own tongue and choking on it. This brought on the heartbeat again. He scanned the stream, fixing and darting his field of vision on all the possible spots where the cormorant might emerge. What type of cormorant is this at all that it can stay down that long? Doesn't it have lungs the same as me?

He heard an unmerciful splash that slapped through

the quietness of the ravine, in an unexpected spot of the water. The cormorant emerged, as if a hand was pushing it up underneath the surface and stabilising it. Two black wings stretched wide with sharp feathers that dripped silver beads of river. The full span must have been the length of his leg. There was a plump tumescent trout thrashing in the cormorant's beak. The cormorant's eye was bright green and round like a wound. Cait was now pointing at the bird and shouting 'Gack, gack' in her high pitch, delight and excitement on her face. The cormorant hopped on to a rock. Through the splashing and Cait's shouts he saw and heard the trout's tail thud off the rock, its mouth gaping in a steady rhythm like it was trying to drink the air. The fish was drowning in the same air that he was tasting in his mouth. The cormorant pinned the trout with the talons on its left foot and pierced its beak into the slimy skin of the creature until it stopped being alive. It celebrated the killing with a clacking noise from its throat. When Cait shouted, the bird paused and then resumed. This terrified him to his core. Blood that was bloodier than blood oozed on the stone and diffused into the water. The cormorant pincered its beak around the fish's robust torso, muscular and firm, and then bit through it until the trout was severed in two. Cait pointed more and screamed 'Gack', drawing attention to herself.

In that moment he jolted to his feet and grabbed Cait under her armpits from behind. Her doll was clasped in her hands, its hair dangled. Her mouth gaped into a silent maw. She searched for a noise and then let out a mighty cry that changed in pitch as he dragged her away. He pulled her towards his chest and ran with her into the mud hut. 'It's okay, it's okay, it's okay,' he said. Cait squirmed under his arm. In a panic, he used his free hand and raised the doll to his mouth. He gripped his front teeth around the fabric of its blue dress and pulled, revealing a sparse wooden skeleton. He situated the doll on the bed of straw where he and Cait had slept, and furrowed the indentation of a miniature crib. He exited the hut backwards. Tears were tracking down her skin as he glared at the stiff dummy boy in the straw that would bide them some time with the fairies.

Outside, Cait wailed through the ravine. Her muscles had tensed with fear, and she stretched out her limbs in a star shape against his chest. The cormorant was still eating the trout on the rock. He shouted at the bird, 'Hey, hey, look at me.' Cait faced outward, his hands under her arms. He kicked at the churn. The tin buckled down the centre and stuck on his boot. He shook it off, and the contraption crumbled into a heap. He fell back on the grass, but held Cait so that she didn't make contact. His toe was sore. He got up. He turned to the eight bottles of poitín with the peg of his boot and knocked them all towards the stream with frantic swipes of his legs. Some spilled out on the grass, others plopped under the ripples of the stream. Their milky essence blended with the water and the ghosts of the barley dispersed back into the land. He was certain that the cormorant saw this.

Cait was now bawling loudly. He ran into the stream and generated big splashes with his knees. Trout dispersed in all directions away from him. He held Cait high above his head and screamed an animal scream at the cormorant, a scream from the bottom of his guts where the pain lived, as if to make himself sound bigger than he was. The cormorant flew off over the hazel trees and left the bloodied trout on the rock.

He turned Cait around into a hug and held her firmly and lovingly with both arms around her, hoisting her higher up his chest than usual, so that her head lay over his shoulder. Her pink, swollen face sobbed and gasped intermittently as she watched the poitín still in bits behind them. He would explain this day to her when she could understand it.

No smell to follow or tracks to trace. He waded deeper into the river until it reached his stomach and never touched her feet. They both moved with the current and blended with the flow upstream until they exited the ravine. His heart was dancing inside his ribs. Steam rose from his clothes like a horse and he stared out at the moor. He told the blue mountains that he would figure something else out and begged for their protection. Cait's bum nestled in his arm, his hand secured her back, with her head resting over his shoulder. She slept with the movement and a little brown curl from her neck blurred into his vision. He told himself that he would kill or die for just one of those curls.

I'll Give You Barcelona

I do this thing in the gym in the gym locker room. Not just me. Men do this thing in the gym locker room. We try to be as naked as possible at all times. To show other men how much of a confident Alpha Male you are.

You'll see the opposite with the younger men. Less sure of themselves, trainee men. Lads of about eighteen or nineteen, they always have their towels around their tackle. Swimming shorts in the shower too, which is a real taboo. I don't take too much heed of it. They're allowed to be like that. They're not silverbacks yet. In fact, it's a show of respect to us.

But a grown man in swimming shorts? Like me? Well into my forties. You'd better be heading to the pool immediately after your shower. Because swimming shorts make the other men think, 'Are you saying I want to be looking at your dick? Why are you hiding it from me like I want to see it? Show it to me so I can ignore it.'

So we get violently naked. It's a staring contest with no staring. And if my deodorant falls on the tiles, I'm bending over. I'm perching down and picking it up and you might have to deal with my arsehole. That's just how it is. Because I'm not about to be alpha-maled by these other cunts, so there's my fucking langer too while we're here, dangling from behind. Live with it.

And the more alpha a man is, the more likely he is to draw his leg up on a bench and towel his barse in front of the other men. He'll slide the towel through his crack and make a bannister out of himself. And he might shout and scream about a holiday or a dead relative while he's doing it, so you have to pay attention to him. You counter this by mastering the art of looking through his nudity. You never look away. Fuck me, you never ever turn away. You'd have to kill yourself. And you can hear the wet smacks of his parted arse if he's near you. Double points to him if you taste the spice of his taint in the humid air.

Silent nudity is almost as bad as swimming shorts in the shower. Your body must be made the centre of attention, while other men force themselves to watch everything around you. Draw them into your equipment until their bodies are orbiting you. Be the sunshine made of beige flab. That's real leadership.

'Did you know that Bruce Lee was so healthy his heart burst?'

When I've had a good day of fares in the taxi, when the arse would feel like someone else's from sitting down, I'll hit the gym to get the blood pumping around my veins again. I get stuck into the lifting I does. I take it seriously, and I take my health seriously. Cause I'm not hitting fifty and turning into one of these cunts who looks like a continental quilt. Nothing distracts me from lifting. But recently I've started getting into them podcasts while I'm lifting. I heard the younger lads talking about them and said I'd give them a go. I was listening to a podcast about cheetahs last week. While I was tearing through the last reps of the fourth set on the bench. I'd been doing progressive overload. It's where you stack the weights on the bar, do a few sets, then add more weight. You keep adding to it, until you can't lift any more. It fatigues the muscles and triggers your glycogen stores. It takes a long time before you see the results. But Rome was a building a day.

I was flat on my back, holding 120kg above my eyes when the fella in my ears says, 'Men come from the plains of Africa. That's where our brains still think we are.'

It kicked me in the mind. I held the bar above my face for too long. I felt the triceps on my right arm lock, and the bar came down on my Adam's apple. Trapped under it, I was. I didn't even try to push it off, I was too focussed on the podcast. The iron of the barbell was so close to my nose that it smelled like the blood of an enemy. If I were on my own I'd be dead, choked out. But Cozzy and Pavel came over and lifted the bar off my neck. They had big pink faces on the pair of them, veiny heads like boners, screaming at me, with spit coming out and all. They looked frightened – that meant they could smell my testosterone.

'Jacky Jacky, are you all right?' I think they said, because I couldn't hear 'em through the big noise-cancelling headphones, and I didn't want to hear 'em either.

'Shut up I'm listening to cheetahs,' I said, even though I wasn't. I was only listening to a fella talking about cheetahs. But that doesn't matter.

I came up off the bench, leaving a sweat stain in the shape of myself that some other prick could wipe off. Because Jacky Kinsella never had to wipe down no benches in here. Cozzy and Pavel had the look of lads who expected a thank you. I alpha-maled them both, by turning my back and walking over to the quieter area near the women's fitness bikes.

I swear though, this podcast lads, this podcast had my undivided attention. I was staring myself out of it in the gym mirror, but I wasn't looking at me. I was looking through me, I was looking at my thoughts, and my right tricep was spasming like a drowning rat.

It was an interview with an ex-Navy SEAL called Corey Shunt who'd lived with cheetahs in Africa. Every day he'd go down to the tree where the cheetah pack were, and every day they'd growl at him and show their teeth. Until one day, he drugged a meerkat and bit into its neck in front of them. Freaked them all out. The cheetah pack accepted him as one of their own. They respected him and they feared him. He hacked their minds. He stayed with the lanky yellow fuckers for a full year and all. Then he flew home to Miami and wrote a book about how we should all be living like cheetahs. And that's why he was being interviewed on this podcast.

Humans have it wrong, he said, with our office jobs and our polo necks and our hot dinners. Instead, we should eat one giant raw meal a week – offal, cartilage, bone marrow – and spend the rest of the week running and lifting like we hunted it ourselves. This hacks our minds into thinking that we are cheetahs and that we live in the wild outside of society. He said it can get rid of stress, obliterate worries, make you afraid of nothing. Most importantly, you'll gain the respect of other men. Back to our wild state, before all this shit that we have now. A big empty cheetah head on you. Living in the moment and nowhere else. Like a fucking Buddhist monk on speed.

This was powerful information. The women's area smelled like a leaky attic. There were no women. I grabbed a pair of 40kg dumb-bells in each fist and burst into five sets of Bulgarian split squats with my left foot up on a yoga ball. It works the hamstrings and feels like twenty bouncers headbutting you in the arse. And it'll burn the palms of your hands too, even with weightlifting gloves on. But you won't see results if you don't feel the pain. As the man says, a burden of hands is worth chewing a bush.

Corey Shunt had my mind scooting off in all sorts of directions. Imagining how I was going to eat my way through an entire butchered calf in one week. Where would I get one? Does raw meat not have you shitting through the eye of a needle? I checked my form in the mirror. It was perfect. My knee bent at a

90-degree angle to my chest, and my glute was poked out to maximise the contraction.

I was doing diaphragmatic breathing with each rep to oxygenate my blood too. I read about it off the back of a creatine tub. Pure loud breathing with sucky lips and bits of spit coming out on the exhale. This and the podcast had me thinking very deep thoughts. Like, my spit spat on my reflection in the mirror, and in each bit of spit there was another reflection of me. Loads of different types of me in the spit mirrors. Tiny little round globs. Up and down, up and down. I watched myself squatting in the mirror spit, moving all wonky, like I was a long streak of bubblegum being stretched out of a child's teeth. I was all, what do they call it? Distortured. My body was all distortured and elastic in the bits of spit. And it reminded me of the dream about the dog.

Sometimes I have a dream about peeling all the skin off my body and wrapping it around a dog. And then the dog attacks a load of strangers in a supermarket. But it's a dog wrapped in my skin, so it looks like a wonky version of me. I see all the people in the supermarket panicking in different directions, and they're down below, because I'm watching from the roof of a multi-storey car park, with no skin on, all red like a fella in a medical book. And the dog who's wearing my skin looks up at me, with my face over a dog's face, and he wants to eat the meat version of me. But I'm not afraid. I want to fuck the dog's mouth. And I wake up in an awful state.

On the last set of the Bulgarian squats, I didn't give myself any rep limit. I kept going until failure. When you do that, it trains the highest possible number of your muscle fibres. It felt like the passion of Christ all the way up the back of my knee as far as my hole. But I tolerated the agony of it when Corey Shunt started calling bullshit on the idea of the Alpha Male. A so-shall construct, he said it was. I felt like this podcast was made for me and me alone. I was Moses talking to the mad bush. Listening to Corey Shunt tell me that the Alpha Male was based on faulty evidence about packs of wolves in zoos. Society is our zoo. We trap ourselves with polo necks and office jobs. This notion of a supreme pack leader who fights his way to domin-ance to lead all the other wolves. It's lies. That only happens in captivity with mentally ill wolves.

'There's no such thing as an alpha wolf in the wild,' he said. And then he went on, flooring me with his knowledge.

'We should forget about wolves altogether. Stop talking about wolves. Shut up about 'em. They're all dead for a reason and the smart ones have turned into dogs. Forget about being an Alpha Male too. Be like a cheetah. Cheetahs don't have a pack leader. There's no alpha in a cheetah pack because all the males are sigmas. They're out running around in the wild. They come and go as they please. Be a Sigma Male. A Sigma Male can have it all. Have your power, your freedom, your pick of the gant.

'But do it independently, don't be concerning yourself with dominating other men. Strike on your own terms and avoid open conflict or posturing. Transcend status and occupy a higher spectrum of dominance,' he said. 'That's the cheetah mindset.'

This fella was smart. And I was agreeing with him. My head nearly fell off, I was nodding so much. Sure, how could we all be the Alpha Male? Wouldn't it end in bloodshed? We'd all be dead by now. Where the fuck was Corey Shunt when I was in my twenties? I needed to hear this back then. Sigma cheetah mindset all the way. This was gonna be my new thing.

I'd gone a bit overboard with the final reps of the Bulgarian squats and could feel a cramp coming on in my hamstring. You never want a cramp in your hamstring in the gym. Because then you've to do a stretch that makes you look like a woman getting ridden on a snooker table at a hen party.

To avoid that, you walk away from the squat and imagine that you're a small baby with a dirty nappy instead. Waddle around a bit. Make your knees rubbery so the muscle fibres can breathe. Fair enough, it looks a bit silly. But then you take the attention away from your legs by swinging your arms in circles and talking pure loud. Distract anyone who's looking, move their eyes up from your legs towards your torso and head. Doesn't matter what you're talking about either.

So I started talking about cheetahs. I swung my arms like a windmill and looked at a fella doing pull-ups. Stared right into his eyes and shouted, 'Big, long, yellow cunts from Africa with sharp teeth.'

I said it like a question too. I don't know why I did, but your man didn't finish his set anyway. He'd his mouth open like he wanted to talk but couldn't find the words. He got pure nervous because I had just dominated him. I asked myself, was that the smartest move? Would a sigma cheetah have done that? Or am I naturally just too much of an alpha wolf? The journey of taming myself had begun.

At this point of the podcast, I'd left the gym floor and headed for the changing rooms and decided I was going to have a swim in the pool to cool down my muscles after the workout. I have a ritual. The second I cross the threshold of the changing room, I immediately get nude. No exceptions.

Corey Shunt was now talking about how to boil an egg by shouting at it, and I was giving his words my full undivided attention. Which was a mistake in hindsight. I should have put the phone in the locker and taken the big headphones off when I stripped. Because my body was going to the pool, but my mind was heading for a shower. I forgot to put on my swimming shorts and walked cock-first into the public pool. Which wasn't Alpha Male or confident or independent or nothing, it's a fucking sex crime.

Luckily, it was quiet at 11 a.m. so there was only one other person in the pool. But that person was Purple Brosnan.

I hate Purple Brosnan. A bread delivery man in his mid-fifties who only wore shoes from TK Maxx so you'd think he was a millionaire. He was a four-foot-tall upside-down traffic cone with acne scars on his shoulders and swollen toes from years of injecting steroids into them. He smelled like bleach. Cock of the walk in the gym because there's a little trophy beside the vending machines with his name on it. He'd won a few bodybuilding competitions in his time, and you could tell by the way he'd clench his arse cheeks that he thought he was better than you because of it. I hated his arse as well. It looked like a photograph of a roast chicken.

And now there he was, taking off his swimming goggles to witness my naked body. The bottom half of him was under the water so he had wobbly stumps instead of legs. He squinted, and that made his head look like a bag of chips. He wasn't one bit intimidated by my nudity. The shock must have given me a mickey like a belly button because he stared clean at it with disgust in his vinegary eyes, then up at my noise-cancelling headphones, and then back down at my cock again. I could see his mouth moving.

'What the fuck are you doing, Jacky?'

'I'm listening to cheetahs,' I said.

Wrong answer again. I slid the headphones off to try to explain myself, but I wasn't thinking straight, so I rested them around my neck like a collar. Bad move. Any chance of saving myself was gone as soon as I felt my face going red. Then I did the worst thing imaginable. I cupped my two hands over my dinner like I was in a penalty shoot-out.

And Purple Brosnan, the little bastard, gets up out of the pool with his 2007 TK Maxx Armani flip-flops slapping on the tiles. He walks past me, no eye contact, and whispers in a managerial tone: 'Put on some shorts, Jacky. They do children's swimming classes in here.'

The bollix thought I came into the pool with my flute out to alpha-male him, and now he'd just alpha-maled me. He'd won. Purple Brosnan won. I can't have Purple Brosnan thinking he alpha-maled me. Even though I'm not doing this Alpha Male shit no more, but still, he doesn't know that. As far as he's concerned he just won.

Fuck the podcast now. I dropped the headphones on the poolside and barrelled back into the changing rooms and made myself as nude as possible. I had a go at it all. I held my breath to inflate my chest. I walked with my legs parted like I'd shat myself. I had sex with the air in front of me so that my langer slapped against my thigh. I spread my toes as far as they'd go. I launched my elbows out, pretending I was dragging the corpses of two dead horses behind me. Demanding respect through all the skin on me. The room was chubby with undressed men. I imposed myself on them, but it was no use. Something had gone sour. Whatever way

Purple Brosnan had cucked me in that swimming pool had changed my status – the weakness rose out of my pores, and every man could taste it in the vapour. I'd been too emotional with my body.

Cozzy was over by the hairdryers palming lavender oil into Pavel's delts, neither of 'em even acknowledged how naked I was. I made that noise that you make after coming out of a steam room to let men know that the steam in the steam room was very steamy: 'Huuuuaaaaaahhh.'

Nothing. Ignored. Whole place stinking of lavender and barse.

Then Cozzy says, 'Where are your big headphones gone, Jacky? Are you not listening to cheetahs any more?'

And Pavel, with his darting eyes, did a sharty chuckle, looking for allies, a smirk you wouldn't see the like of on a ferret. He was testing the electricity to see if it was okay to jeer. There was a coward's silence.

And then Purple Brosnan, the mahogany bollix, pushes his head out from a locker door and pinches his wrinkly prick in his fingernails and says, 'Jacky's off banging cheetahs up the arse and then running around the swimming pool nude with a dirty bell-end full of cheetah shit, looking for a nine-year-old to sniff it.'

All the men did these hungry laughs that grew louder against the ceramic of the walls. Even the bony fella with the cleft palate who has tits from playing golf. No one knew his name, he wasn't worth a name, and he was howling at me. I felt like the World Trade Center getting a slap off a plane and crumbling on Sky News.

A softer part of me wanted to tell them the truth. That I'd been so distracted by a life-changing podcast about cheetahs that I'd walked into the swimming pool naked by accident. But you couldn't open up like that. No more than you could openly acknowledge the nudity hierarchy.

Corey Shunt spoke about this on the podcast, though. This is what happens to the alpha wolf in captivity. They respect you, they fear you, they give you first dibs on the barbells. But the second you show weakness, they all turn on you at once. The alpha wolf is banished from the pack, forced to wander the perimeters alone and die beside the fence, or to cancel his gym membership. That's the beauty and cruelty of nature.

They were still laughing. Not the big loud laughs, but the smaller bent-over chuckles that sound like a nose getting blown. My eyesight became wobbly and my forehead hurt with rage. Laughing at Jacky Kinsella in the gym changing rooms, are they? Have they gotten me confused with a man who lets other men laugh at him? I kept my head stuck in my locker so they couldn't see any emotion out of me.

To calm myself down, I stared at the photograph of toes on my athlete's foot powder. They were slender toes, and I couldn't tell if it was a woman's toes or a small man's toes that had been shaved. And when I thought about shaving the hair off the knuckle of a toe, I felt my face getting less red and my jaw unclenching. I could have picked up the bottle, held it up for all to see, pointed at the toes, and said to Purple Brosnan something like, 'Look at these gorgeous toes. They wouldn't put your big Chernobyl toes on this bottle of athlete's foot powder, you geriatric club-footed cunt.' And then he would have been the one who was being laughed at. And I would have restored my status. But I didn't. Because I'm not doing this alpha wolf shit no more, I'd decided that in the mirror earlier. I have the sigma cheetah mindset now. I think before I act.

The laughter ended and the time had come for us all to hit the showers. Conversation turned to Aston Villa and the actor Michael Douglas who got tonsil cancer from licking a fanny. No one asked for my input, because there was too much tension. They were all waiting for my response to Purple Brosnan.

Was Jacky just going to let him castrate him like that, they were thinking. Jacky Kinsella? Jacky, who had trials for Everton, Jacky? Jacky Kinsella who has his own gym locker that wasn't really mine, but everyone knew it was mine? Was he really going to bow down to Purple?

I took out my big red Bermuda swimming shorts from my locker and slid them on over my nudity. Pavel suckled at his post-workout protein shake like it was a tit. Cozzy threw a glance at me the way you'd watch a car crash, his voice gone up into his throat like a child, 'Are you not coming into the showers, Jacky? We're all showering now.'

'I am,' I said. 'Did you not see me benching 120kg? The pair of ye were barely able to lift it off my neck. I'm stinking. Why would you think I'm not coming into the shower?'

Every man gawked at the white tropical flowers on my swimming shorts with terror and pity in their eyes. And I let them have that little moment. Like a fucking cheetah in the long grass over a swarm of antelope. Purple Brosnan stood silent with his tanned prick out.

They say actions be louder than words. Well, I'd a

plan to fuck with the rules a bit. Get inside their heads. You see, you've to be a bit more protective of your nudity in the shower because showers are sexual. Be nude, but not as nude as the changing room. Let everyone see that you've got nothing to hide. But don't be swinging anything around. Nothing that might risk your wet skin touching another man's wet skin.

You play it forward in the changing room, you defend in the showers. Arses to the wall. Feet nailed to the tiles, chests out. You can't enjoy it, washing needs to be functional. Make noises like the shower is attacking you. When the hot water hits the back of your shoulders, pull the wet over your front like a rucksack with your fists.

Too much lather is weakness. Ideally, use water only and avoid shower gel. Let your skin resist the droplets, and you look impenetrable. The 'no soap in the showers' thing is bullshit – soap is actually better than shower gel, because you can hit someone with soap. But bare water is best.

No turning away, stare through the nudity. Don't ever spend any great length of time washing your dick, in case you get a sponty. Flaccid is leadership.

Talk if you want, but if you do talk, make a solid point with your words. Shout. Don't let any man think you're talking just to distract yourself from looking at his shaft.

And of course, the most important rule of all, don't ever wear swimming shorts.

The showers smelled like the inside of a hotel kettle. Perfectly square room full of tiles. A fucking shower, like. Six shower heads and then a drain in the middle, which was no man's land. If there were more men than six men, then two men had to share (no touching), depending on the man.

Jacky Kinsella never had to share a shower head with any man – you get the point.

There were six of us. Cozzy, Pavel, Golf Tits, some other fella with freckles who thought he was above it all (he wasn't), and me in my swimming shorts.

Purple Brosnan was fashionably late, because all of us knew that this shower would be his coronation. He was gonna pull some shit, some big alpha move. Those were the rules. After dressing me down in the pool, and then that joke in the locker room, and now me wearing swimming shorts. He had to take his crown. Under those shower heads was where he'd decapitate me. In front of witnesses to legitimise it.

The warm water was teeming from the walls. Sounded like a leaky garage in a storm. Pavel was first to try and burst the tension. Rubbing soap into his neck and choking himself, he yelped, 'My legs are fucked from them new deadlifts.'

'Eat a banana after to replenish your glycogen stores,' says Cozzy.

And then a thundery roar came in: 'We all know where Pavel wants to stick that banana, he wants to ram it up his Latvian jacksie, hahahah.'

No one laughed. It was Purple Brosnan, gliding into the shower, barefoot, two inches shorter, with the chest out and the chin up. I watched him on the sly. With all due respect, he'd a body like stone, a little ball-peen hammer of a man. He was streaky with that dark fake tan that bodybuilders wear, and the brown dripped off his swollen toes and dissolved into the water and made it rusty. I hated the bones of him. He made eye contact with no one and pulled out a small blue plastic disposable razor. Held it up with the gristly elbows above his forehead. Every cunt glanced at me for the split of a second. That was a solid move in fairness, even I got a bit of a fright when I saw the razor.

'I've a competition in a month, ye don't mind if I shave in here,' he says.

'We're not allowed to shave in the shower for hygiene reasons,' says Golf Tits.

Be quiet, Golf Tits, stay out of it.

Purple asked again, a bit quieter and directed at the real men.

'Ye don't mind if I shave, lads. I'm putting on a second coat of the tan after the shower and I need to clear away some hair.'

'Go ahead, Purple,' says Cozzy. 'Where are you competing?'

And Purple goes, 'Over in Barcelona.'

Now, we'd all assumed that Purple wanted to shave his chest or legs. But before anyone could even take in his words, he faced the wall, and very rapidly bent over. With one set of fingers, he tore apart his arse cheeks, and with the other, he used the razor to shave the curly auburn hairs that circled his hoop. He dug into it. One lad actually gasped. Golf Tits flat out left.

Purple Brosnan pointed his arsehole at every single man in the shower. Holding the room hostage. They immediately turned their backs and washed themselves pure quickly with anxious uncomfortable fidgets. They hadn't the status to witness what he was doing to his anus. These were the advanced tactics of a veteran. He was in full control. Big alpha move.

'Oh Barcelona, I'd say that's lovely this time of year,' squealed Cozzy into the wall, like an excited woman.

Purple Brosnan started screaming while he was shaving.

'Oh ya, it's an over-50s bodybuilding competition. I've a fair shot at gold or silver. Dorian Yates is on the adjudicating panel. I'll be cutting out carbs completely next week. Three chickens a day and a yard of broccoli.'

And then he pivoted his little half-shorn hoop at me. I stared at his arse like it was a High Court judge. I despised his undercarriage. A crinkly cyclops balloon-knot rectum. Tanned glutes divided by a big stupid long magnolia barse, ending in a pair of continental quilt balls. And about nine grey pubes.

'What do you think, Jacky?' his ring winked when he talked. 'Do you reckon I'll win a trophy in Barcelona?'

This was the barrel of the gun to my temple.

'I'll give you Barcelona,' I said.

Which didn't make any sense at all, but before I could even feel embarrassed about it, I was biting down on his left arse cheek. I was giving him Barcelona with my mouth. Then it made sense. I hadn't planned it. Nature did it. I latched on to his hole, my nostril in his ring and all. It smelled like a line of coke.

I kept my swimming shorts on. I transcended status and floated to a higher spectrum of dominance.

'Jackaaaaay, Jackaaayy, stoppppp,' they all started screaming.

Because they could hear my testosterone. I thought about starting a war. I thought about starting a podcast. I hung from the back of Purple Brosnan. I didn't draw blood, but I left a mark.

'Ahhhhhhhh,' he shouted.

In that moment I realised I wasn't the alpha wolf, and I wasn't the sigma cheetah either. I was that skin-covered dog from my dream whose mouth I want to fuck.

Pamela Fags

Noel Riordan's silver hair had gone yellow from neglect. Every Friday, he arrived to me in the same suit. A sandy tweed job with a rip on the shoulder, biscuit-green shirt underneath. It looked like it was the only suit he had ever owned. Very pointy leather shoes. Today he dragged a streak of green farmyard shit in on top of my fire-retardant carpet. I left it there. He was forever tonguing his false teeth around in his mouth as a nervous tic. Sometimes I'd look up at him and his teeth were upside down. And when he'd sit across from me, I'd stoop over to reach his documents. His eyes would be on me. He didn't have any finger-nails for some reason. I hated representing him. But he never objected when I smoked cigarettes in my office; he liked the smell, and said that he used to be a hoor for the cigarettes before they put the stent in his heart.

I enjoyed listening to the names of the greyhounds that he brought up too, names like Seaside Trembler,

Ultan's Comet and Douggie's Comeuppance. He was attempting to sue the Limerick Greyhound Association, who had banned him from entering competitions. His dogs had failed drug tests and showed high amounts of caffeine in their blood. He'd slam his fist down on his thigh and shout things like, 'Archie's Bracket was a fucker for tea bags and you couldn't keep the bitch out of a kitchen bin. Am I to have my reputation as a dog man varnished for that?' I'd have to swivel my chair around and bury my face in a filing cabinet to hide my smirk. It was the type of case that could last two years and still go nowhere. He was driven by a loss of face, and those were the clients who paid the bills. Before he'd leave my office, he'd take off his little cap with the sausage fingers of his disgusting red hands and ask me to go over across the road to Neesons Hotel for a toasted sandwich and a glass of sherry with him. 'I couldn't possibly tarnish our professional relationship with romance, Noel. I look forward to seeing you next week,' I'd say. 'I suppose you're right, Pamela,' he'd say back. He'd leave my office with the head down. From behind, his bald patch reminded me of a dog's anus.

Earlier that day, my brother Brendan rang me. He was putting a deposit on a suit in order to go to a wedding next Saturday. As was always the case with my family and any type of formal occasion, it became very dramatised and I got quite involved in it unnecessarily. He said the wedding was for some cunt of an architect who's marrying a lesbian, so he's coming into the city centre to pick out the suit. I asked him how he knew the bride was a lesbian and he said, 'I've no phone credit, can I come to your office or not?' This meant that the bride was an ex-girlfriend and the architect was a friend who didn't know that he hated him.

Brendan had one of those mad red heads of curly hair and he looked like a circus clown at the best of times. If I'm being honest, I'm afflicted with the same appearance. My whole family are. Brendan was sixteen years older than me, well into his fifties. I loved him dearly, but when he came in my office door, he puffed back his shoulders and strutted around the carpet in a judgemental performance, scanning the mess of papers and boxes of files like it was my old bedroom and I was still a teenager. He picked up the coffee mug on my desk that was full of mould, and when he put it back down, a puff of green spores rose up and landed all powdery on a pile of documents that I kept on the floor. I didn't care. I could tell by the way his lips pursed that he was thinking of teasing me. But he chose not to, because he was unemployed and was currently standing in my office, which I own. He took one of the Benson & Hedges from the packet on my desk. He only ever smoked when he was in my company. I expected him to have nosy questions about Noel the dog man who fed tea bags to greyhounds, like he usually does, but he coughed and said, 'How in the fuck are you a solicitor and you can't even clean up the fag butts from your windowsill? Do your clients not complain?' 'They can go fuck themselves,' I said. We laughed so hard that I heard the single-glazed windowpane vibrate. He told me about his morning.

He had gone to an outlet store to put a deposit on a suit for the cunt of an architect's wedding. They're OK suits, but you know, it's an outlet store, so something is bound to be off. The suits could be old or damaged. They might just be out of fashion. Anyway, he parked in a multi-storey car park close to the outlet store, and as he was exiting, his eye caught a crisp fifty euro note beside the ticket machine. So he was like, Fucking excellent, fifty euro, the sun is shining on Brendan today. I'm going to use this fifty euro to put a deposit on a new suit in the outlet store. One of the good ones. So he did, and he was telling me all about the wonderful suit that he picked out and how he put down a deposit for this suit and how he's going to buy it next week. I'm so pleased with this suit. It's a Hugo Boss suit, an incredibly discounted Hugo Boss suit, but still a Hugo Boss suit and so on and so on. I told him that Hugo Boss suits were actually designed for the Nazis. He didn't like this. He took more cigarettes from my packet, and we both flicked our ashes on the floor. My office was thick with smoke, it was like the 1960s. Brendan was so animated and giddy when he told the story. I had one client after, but I considered cancelling on her and asking my brother to go day-drinking with me over in Charlie Malone's pub. Because I really do love him, he's hilarious.

He began telling me again all about the fifty euro that he found, with such a glow on his face, like this was the most important thing to ever happen to him. But then I said, 'You found this fifty euro on the ground. But did you ask anybody in the car park if they dropped it? Maybe that fifty euro was incredibly important to somebody and they might have been in your immediate vicinity and you could have found the owner, but you didn't, you only thought of yourself?' The joy dropped from his eyes and he let the cigarette burn longer in his hand. 'I didn't think of that, Pamela,' he said. 'There's a client coming shortly and I have to open the windows, so you'll need to go. Maybe think about what you've done,' I said. He left. I peeked my head over the mug with all the mould and wondered if those spores could make me sick.

My job was easy and my office was a cramped pack of shit that I never cleaned. It didn't bother me. It was above a Subway. The smell of sandwiches made my clients hungry and they'd want to leave early. I only ever accepted the type of clients who should be bringing their problems to a psychoanalyst. The fallout from a divorce, for instance. Or daughters who have such heated arguments with their mothers at Christmas time that their mother shakes them or slaps them, so the daughter asks me to litigate against their own mother. But really, deep, deep down, what they want is their mother's approval, they just don't know it. I'll take neighbours who have a dispute about a boundary fence and a tree. I eat those cases with no salt. It's always men, and the litigious man is usually jealous of the other man's wife. '*In compliance with common law principles, it is incumbent upon you to prevent your flora from extending on to neighbouring premises. I urge you to rectify this matter promptly by ensuring the overgrowth is pruned back within a 30-day period. In the event of non-compliance, my client shall be compelled to pursue legal remedies, which may include, but are not limited to, seeking damages and an injunction for nuisance. Your prompt action is highly recommended to avert unnecessary legal proceedings.'* I'll make three hundred quid a pop for that class of fart talk. Back and forth with some other solicitor for as long as we like. It will never see a court. I could solve all the world's problems if I just told people the truth.

It was Friday afternoon. Noel Riordan sat across from me teary-eyed, revolving his dentures in his mouth. Unshaven today. Silver stubbly jowls like a gang of teenagers had vandalised his face with car paint. 'Bastards. Bastards. Bastards.' He was shouting it in a whisper. He spat old-man spit on my fire-retardant carpet. I didn't care. And when he said 'Bastard', the esses spluttered through his teeth. 'Have they forgotten that I'm the dog man who reared Hanley's Fiasco from a pup? What need had I to drug those powerful beasts with caffeine? And what about Dunphy's Bunting and Dolmio Hairstyles, the two spotted twins?' He continued. 'I practically tit-fed that litter and wasn't their mother half a spastic? Wasn't she? Wasn't she?' He said that bit directly at me like I'd know the answer. I imagined his two long geriatric nipples and swivelled my chair around again with the giggles. 'All champion dogs,' he went on. 'All champion dogs. And those Bastards have the nerve to disrespect me like they did? Cyril Tynan and his puppets on the committee. Bastards.' 'We'll have our day in court with them, Noel,' I said. Knowing full well that we won't.

I lit another cigarette and Noel licked his lips when the smoke left my mouth, and he followed the plume up to the big yellow stain on my polystyrene ceiling tiles. 'Will we send them another letter, Pamela?' he enquired. 'Oh, I'll be sending very strongly worded letters, Noel. I will serve another notice to formally communicate the severity of the issue, your determination to assert your rights, and our intent to take the fullest legal action if a satisfactory response and resolution are not achieved.' He salivated at me like I was a carvery lunch. Noel then informed me that he had been refused access to Limerick Greyhound Stadium last night, effectively banning him from even attending a greyhound meet as a spectator. Which was a little harsh, in fairness, and it might even constitute actual grounds for a court case if I was willing to put that type of work in. It was the last straw he said, he won't be responsible for his actions he said, he has a Civil War revolver buried in a condom full of grease he said.

The last bit was whispered like he wanted to impress me, and it did impress me, but I wouldn't let him see it. I took in a judgemental breath, sighed, and reminded him that he was in the presence of a solicitor. I instructed him to refrain from unilateral action, as this dispute must be approached within the purview of the established legal framework. He swallowed and said, 'I suppose you're right, Pamela.' I could tell that he enjoyed it when I scolded him like that. He stared down with self-pity at his terrifyingly swollen hands and told me that he had named a colleague's grey-hound after me, and I said, 'Excuse me, Noel?' 'I did,' he replied, 'Dinny Ryan has a promising pup, and she needed a name so I christened her Pamela Fags.' 'Pamela Fags?' I said. 'Yes, you've been so helpful to me, Pamela, sending off those letters to the Bastards, the Bastards above in that committee, and putting the fear of God into them. You deserve it. She has her first race tomorrow night. And she's a fine cur too. There'll be a champion in her yet.' He said this with a very seri-ous expression of certainty. I won't lie. I was unbeliev-ably flattered that Noel had named a greyhound in my honour, even if a separate part of me sensed that it was a new attempt to get me to the hotel with him. But when he left this time, he didn't even ask me to go to the hotel, he just kept repeating, 'Cyril Tynan will pay. We'll get the Bastards. We'll have our day in court,' while clasping his palms around my fingers like they were an injured bird that he was trying to euthanise. There was a strength in his bloodshot eyes and I wondered if I'd have let him seduce me if he were forty years younger.

I closed the door and was shook with a sudden desire to clean my office. But when I sconced over the mess, it ceased to be a clutter of physical things and instead became a feeling of hopelessness followed by murderous anger. Buckled folders over stacks of memos and depositions with withery ears. The whole lot slightly yellowed by cigarettes. Butts of different ages everywhere all at once, smoked down to the filter. Fag burns galore. All surfaces and objects dulled with a fine grey powder of ash. Multiple staplers that I thought I had lost. There was one particular Manilla folder that had been rained on after I left a window open. It must have been four years ago. Anyway, the pages inside had formed a single lump of turquoise fungus. It wasn't a folder any more, it was a living thing. It should have been paying me rent. Post-its posted to stacks of papers with notes that I couldn't understand even though I wrote them. Paper clips. Calendars. Newspapers.

Those leaflets that get thrown in the letter box, the charity ones about second-hand clothes, loads of them. Tangled wires from the PC on my desk. Old bird shit from that time with the seagull. Coffee mugs, a fucking hair straightener from Argos. All towered over by overflowing fat bastard filing cabinets behind my desk that I wanted to crush me some day. Among the chaos, a little island of fire-retardant carpet was scooped out where my clients' chair was. I rarely examined the mess in all its constituent parts like this. I wouldn't even know where or how to begin cleaning it. So I sat back in my chair and smoked the absolute bollocks off a Benson & Hedges instead. I relaxed, and I noticed that Noel Riordan had forgotten his tweed jacket and left it hanging around the back of the chair.

There was a loud knock on the door. I went to answer, assuming it was Noel Riordan returning for his jacket. It wasn't Noel Riordan, it was my brother Brendan. He pushed straight past me with a plastic bag in his hand and began smoking my cigarettes. He was uneasy, taking rapid puffs, blowing nostril smoke and tiptoe stepping over the mess on the floor like a flamingo. This is what he proceeded to tell me, in more or less these words. He went back to the outlet store and retrieved his fifty-euro deposit like I had asked him to. I had completely fucking forgotten about all of this if I'm being honest; it was a week ago and I have a job. But anyway, he took the money to the security guard who worked in the multi-storey car park. The security guard looked at him like he had twelve arses and said, 'How in the fuck are we supposed to locate the owner of a fifty euro note? No one reported it missing. It's not in a wallet. There's no ID. It could be anyone's money. It may even have blown in from the road. If you want my advice, pal, just keep it, it's yours, man.' 'That was enough to clear my conscience,' said Brendan. His forehead sweat frizzled his curls and made him appear particularly clown-like. He was still jittery with anxiety, and then he infected me with his anxiety and I said, a bit loud, 'Then what's the problem, Brendan? What are you doing here in my office all upset?' He took another fag from the packet and tried to light it with a stapler. 'I thought it was one of them novelty lighters,' he said. I lit his fag with my fag and called him a useless prick. He went on with his story, recounting it like a little boy.

So he had returned to the outlet store today, and said, 'Hello, I was here last Friday, I'm ready to buy the suit that I put a deposit on, the Hugo Boss one.' And then the outlet store were all, 'We sold the suit, sir. It's gone.' And then Brendan was like, 'But I put a deposit on the suit. You can't sell the fucking suit. I put a deposit on it.' And then they said in response, 'You did put a deposit on it. But then you took the deposit back, and during that time, we sold the suit.' So he was like, 'I know I took the actual fifty euro note, but I still had a deposit on it.' So then they were all, 'That's not how deposits work, sir, but we have another suit that's similar and it's much cheaper. Do you want that instead?' Brendan was awful disappointed, but he swallowed his pride and bought the cheaper suit. That was the end of his formal-wear saga, or so I thought. 'Ah, you got a suit for the wedding, well done,' I said, relieved. 'What's your specific problem then, Brendan? What is bothering you? Why are you here?' We had both worked each other up at this point. Brendan didn't say a word; he stood there with a big serious face on him. He reached into his plastic bag and held the trousers of the suit in the air like they were a severed head and says, 'Sniff that, Pamela, sniff the crotch, sniff it. Tell me I'm not going mad. Go on, sniff that.' He spoke the words in an affected English accent. I knew immediately what was happening. So I buried my face in the gusset of the suit pants and began inhaling. And there it was, the pain in my tummy.

Actually, no. Pause this. Before I continue sniffing the crotch of these suit pants. I need to give you some details about my childhood.

I grew up in a house with four much older brothers. When I was five years of age, they were in their late teens and early twenties. A lot older, so they were forever attending debs. There was a plethora of graduation ceremonies too, maybe a wedding or three. I can't fully recall. Numerous situations where my older brothers had occasion to rent suits or tuxedos. It was a significant part of my early years compared to other children. All incredibly stressful and unnecessarily dramatic events. Instigated and exacerbated by my daddy, God rest him, who was very passionate about stains and odours. He was quite an eccentric man, you could say. My father would become deathly serious when there was a risk of rented formal-wear smelling like someone else's sweat. The sweat of a strange man, so to speak. He had two theories about this, aptly named the first theory and the second theory. One of them I completely agree with. The other one is quite far-fetched and brings the pain to my stomach.

The first theory concerned dry cleaning, which my father didn't consider to be real cleaning at all, because, in his words, the fabric was merely agitated by a solvent as opposed to being deeply cleansed at a molecular level by a detergent. Dry cleaning, he maintained, was a form of masking, which could never truly eliminate the lipids and proteins that were present in human sweat. So if there was even the tiniest hint of another human's sweat on a rented suit or tuxedo, it must be returned. As soon as you put on that suit and attend the formal occasion, you are in serious trouble, he'd say. Especially if you have a couple of pints to heat up the blood, or maybe chance a bit of dancing. The moisture and warmth of your own body will awaken the odour of the previous wearer. The dormant stench blooms with the catalyst of your sweat. You start to really stink. And it doesn't matter how thoroughly you've cleansed your body or how much deodorant you've worn. It's not your sweat, it's someone else's sweat. Now you're the smelly person at the function. You. Smelling like someone else. And that's just the truth of it. There is no acceptable aggregate of another person's sweat that can be permitted to acquiesce in a rented suit or tuxedo. Send it back and demand a fresh one. He'd repeat that throughout my childhood like a mantra to all of my brothers. My father was correct about dry cleaning, however; it can be a risk. But it was his second theory that consumed him.

My father formulated the second theory while watching David Attenborough nature documentaries. He grew tormented by footage of wild animals and how they would mark territory using scents and pheromones. Leveraging this knowledge, he asserted that humans subconsciously glean information about others' mental states, dispositions or personalities through scent and sweat. So if you arrive at a wedding and the suit begins to smell like the sweat of another man, if that man was a bit of a prick, we'll say, or if he was an aggressive man, other people will then act aggressively towards you. You can be as polite as you like, but the sweat will override all rationality. Or worse still, the smell of the other man's sweat can rise up into your own nose, and you will take on aspects of his personality and behave accordingly. All occurring beyond your awareness or control. Absolutely insane stuff. Of course, my mother disagreed. She reasoned that my father always drank too much and would consistently make an arse out of himself at formal occasions, and his theory was just an excuse to avoid accepting responsibility for his drinking. 'You're poisoning your children with nonsense,' she'd scream. And he'd be on the verge of tears with her, howling. 'Then how do you explain the job interview with the porridge people, Marion? Was there any drink taken when I met the porridge people?' Referencing an incident in his thirties where he self-sabotaged a potential role as contamination chemist at Odlums Porridge because he believed his suit had been previously worn by a man with low self-esteem. I don't even think my father had faith in the second theory himself, it was just something he held on to so my mother wouldn't win. He was saving face. This was what I had for a childhood.

My daddy would spend the daytimes dressed in a three-piece suit, cleaning the house impeccably, pretending he wasn't hungover. He'd rub the surfaces down with a rag of industrial alcohol so you couldn't smell it on his breath. My mother waiting to pounce. I would be getting pains in the pit of my belly watching them. I must have been six years old when my youngest brother Andy returned home one evening with a rented tuxedo for his debs. I remember him dragging the smell of cold winter air in the door when it closed. My father used a poker to anxiously molest the fire and waited in the living room with a grave set of eyes on him. I didn't understand how fucking stupid it all was back then. My father used to put on, like, kind of an English accent in these situations. And he'd tap on the coffee table with his wedding ring and he'd say, 'Did you inspect the undercarriage? Did you inspect the undercarriage of those trousers, Andrew? Brandish the garment hither.' Then he would take the suit between the tips of his fingers like it might bite him, and sniff all around the crotch and underarm in a loud performative way that communicated a level of expertise and experience. Puffing his nostrils. We'd all be watching. He'd make us go quiet too. He'd say, 'I'm currently receiving olfactory information and I require serenity.' Which made no sense, who needs silence to smell? All of my brothers staring at him with red clown heads, believing in his theory, waiting for his judgement. 'I need alternative counsel,' he'd say, and the suit was passed along to my brothers in order of age. They would each have their turn snorting at the fabric. Occasionally, the suit was impeccably dry cleaned, and neither my father nor my brothers could agree on whether they detected an odour of sweat or not. Furious arguments arose in these situations, and my mother would get involved. It must be pointed out that she refused to participate in the act of suit-sniffing. Instead, she'd scream, 'You're all mad. I am not smelling that fucking suit. I'll wash it. I'll wash the fucking suit, with hot water and soap. Just stop talking about it.' My father would reject this offer. 'Get the child, bring forth the child,' he'd say, all Dickensian. I was the child. He would hold the crotch of the trousers in front of my nose and instruct me to inhale and report my findings. An extension to his pheromone theory was that I had the most acute sense of smell because I was a child, and as a prepubescent girl, I possessed no context for the odour of adult male perspiration and, thus, could not be enchanted by its persuasive effluvium. His words. All of this meant that my assessment was the final ruling. If I said yes, I can smell something bad, my father and brothers would cheer and my mother would let me know that she expected better from me. If I said no, I smell nothing, my father would be heartbroken and disappear for two days. My mother would scold him and call him a wino. I remember it all being a terrible amount of pressure. I usually lied, depending on who I didn't want to upset that day.

So where was I? Yes, my office. Brendan stood there with a big serious-looking face on him. He reached into his plastic bag and held the pants of the suit in the air like a severed head and said, 'Sniff that, Pamela, sniff the crotch, sniff it. Tell me I'm not going mad. Go on, sniff that.' He spoke the words with the same affected English accent as my father. I knew immediately what was happening. I felt that old funny pain in my stomach. I instinctively began to sniff the crotch of his outlet store suit and searched for testicular musk around the gusset. Sniff, sniff, sniff. But my experience had altered somehow. There was nothing. Not that I couldn't smell sweat specifically, I couldn't smell anything at all. Not a thing. It must be the fags, I thought. The years of smoking fags had done away with my sense of smell. To tell you the truth, I felt a relief. 'I can't smell sweat, Brendan, but if you think you can smell sweat, then return the suit,' I told him. 'I smell balls, Pamela. That's some other fella's balls. Some fucker bought it and then returned it after he had his way with the crotch. A full weekend's worth of balls too. Oldest trick in the book. Them gangsters in the outlet store sold it to me as if it was new,' he whimpered. 'Well then, Brendan, as per the Sale of Goods and Supply of Services Act, 1980, you are legally entitled to return this suit. The fact that the suit is pre-worn is a breach of implied condition under Section 14(2) of the Act, which states that goods sold must be of merchantable quality. Given that the outlet store affirmed the suit was new, this action further constitutes misrepresentation under the Consumer Protection

Act, 2007. Therefore, you have a rightful claim to redress, either in the form of a refund, replacement, or repair.' Brendan crumpled the trousers back into the plastic bag and smoked another one of my cigarettes. I joined him. 'So you'll send them a letter for me?' he said. I laughed. 'If you weren't my brother, I'd happily waste your money, Brendan. Just go back to the shop and demand a brand-new suit that doesn't smell like arseholes or whatever. They'll probably get all embarrassed and will replace it. They might even throw in a little dickie bow.' 'I can't do that,' he said, looking down at my fire-retardant carpet. 'It's half four, the shop is closed for the weekend now, and the cunt of an architect's wedding is tomorrow.' I gestured towards the office door and said, 'Just wear the fucking suit to the wedding, Brendan. Just wear the fucking suit and cop on to yourself. Give the crotch a once over in the sink and go at it with a hairdryer if you're paranoid.' Brendan took on a childlike gait; he looked directly into my eyes and said, 'But Daddy's second theory? What if I take on the personality of the previous wearer and disgrace myself at the wedding in front of my ex?' The pain in my tummy dissolved into anger and I said, 'The man was a roaring alcoholic, Brendan. He was lying to himself, there's no second theory. Wear the

189

suit and go to the fucking wedding, and don't be getting rat-arsed. And whatever you do, don't be ringing Ma about it tonight, she's in her eighties and she doesn't need any more crotch discourse at this hour of her life.' 'You're right, Pamela,' he replied and turned to leave. Before he got to the door, he spotted Noel Riordan's jacket resting on the back of the chair. 'What's that?' he said. 'I could wear that.' 'No, no, no you can't wear that, that's my client's jacket, that's not mine to be giving you.' I inserted myself in Brendan's eyeline and he gaped around me with his red clown's head to see the jacket. 'Why not, Pamela? Which client? The ould dirty fella who feeds tea bags to his greyhounds? Let me wear his suit jacket to the wedding. I'll make a real statement with it.' 'What statement would that make, Brendan?' I said. 'That you've had a nervous breakdown and robbed a pensioner, is it? Fuck off home and wash the suit around the spicy areas,' I told him. We hugged. I left the office shortly after.

The next morning, I took a trip to Tesco to buy two rolls of bin bags, cleaning spray, those yellow sponges with the hard green bit on one side and a packet of disinfectant wipes. I fully intended to get the office into a presentable state. I found myself stunted with that feeling of confusion again. I didn't know how to begin the process. Should I wipe the windows and move on to the mouldy mugs? What if I cleaned the desk first and worked outwards from there? Maybe collect all the cigarette butts before I had a go at anything else? I definitely couldn't hire cleaners, because all of the legal documents strewn around the floor contained confidential information about my clients. It would violate their GDPR if a third party perused them. I sat at my computer and searched for cleaning tutorials on YouTube. The videos were mostly made by American teenagers with magnificent-looking bedrooms. The video I chose was made by a girl called Cassie from Philadelphia. She was 19, she thanked her subscribers, she asked me to follow and told me not to forget to smash that like button. I did. She had a boyfriend named Trayger. They had been on a break but now they were back together. She showed me a montage of Trayger skateboarding over royalty-free ukulele music. I didn't like him, he looked like a cartoon drawing of a pigeon. He was too feminine for me. Her bedroom was super messy but she was going to get it spick and span before Trayger came to visit this weekend. Whore. Her bedroom had pink LED lights on the ceiling and a fish tank. She lived in one of them big Yank McMansions. I grew envious of

her bedroom and her life. She had perfected a declut-
tering technique that involved placing all of her itinerant clothes and objects on the bed in a large pile. This
freed up space on the floor and on her desk. She then
vacuumed and wiped all of the surfaces and sprayed
her pillows with jasmine oil, finally folding away the
clothing until her bedroom looked immaculate. I
hated her. But when I watched the video of Cassie
tidying her bedroom, it satiated my desire to clean the
office. I put my feet up on my desk and smoked cigarettes and stared up at my law degree from the University
of Limerick.

My attention turned to Noel Riordan's suit jacket
that hung limp from the empty chair opposite me.
The torn sandy tweed mesh ravaged by the misery of
time. I thought about sunburnt soldiers in World War
I traversing the yellow deserts of Mesopotamia with
those black and tan guns that looked like leaf blowers.
I thought about young Noel Riordan's beige corduroy
flairs falling around his fawny ankles, having a knee
trembler with a greyhound stadium bint in a red-
bricked piss alley. Mutton-chopped and Brylcreemed.
Beehived, she wore too much Elizabeth Arden. I
smelled it all in my head. I became transfixed with the
desire to snort the oxters of Noel Riordan's jacket. It

no doubt had an acrid hum that could cut through whatever the fags had done to the nose of me. Just one sniff, Pamela. A hero's dose of Noel. I rang Noel on his mobile to tell him that he had left his suit jacket in my office. A man answered who wasn't Noel. It was his son Manus, who told me that Noel had died of a stroke during the night. He told me how much Noel spoke of me and he thanked me for how helpful I was to his dearly departed father. Oh Jesus, Noel. God bless us and save us all.

The wind at Limerick Greyhound Stadium would cut you in two, but Noel's jacket kept my ribs warm. I wore a formal dress underneath, lavender satin. The jacket hung baggy like it had been nestled on my shoulders by a man who was concerned about my temperature. I was dying for a pint. They only served Foster's in plastic glasses. Tina Turner blasted from a loudspeaker high above. I queued up at the bar behind all the greyhound people. They didn't really queue. This was rural money. Tweed-jacketed, pink-shirted old men with hairy ears and Cuban-link gold chains. Grubby wads of cash in their fingers. Younger men with painted-on skinny jeans and extremely large pointy tan leather brogues. The women were cut out much better. Bright colours, pinks and highlighter greens, wearing Irish designers. Heidi Higgins and Caroline Kilkenny. Some of them wore feathered fascinator hats that made their heads look like expensive cakes. I couldn't sport a hat like that with my hair as loud and curly as it was. The greyhound people spoke at a fast country pace so that the collective sound of the crowd was *hoora hoora houla*. But still, not one of them looked in judgement at the oversized tweed jacket that hung raggedy around my shoulders. They probably just thought I was touched in the head. My pint of Foster's tasted like fizzy metal. The thin plastic crumpled and froze my fingers until they stung. The wind didn't help. The drink was so cold that I had to swap it between hands. I held the pint in my left, then reached into the big tweed pocket of Noel's jacket to try and warm my right hand. I grabbed an odd accumulation of papery lumps and yanked out several tea bags. I stared down at them in my palm and put them back. Noel you absolute divil.

There was a flurry of activity when the crowd rushed towards the line of bookies beside the tracks. Red-faced men at kiosks with branding for Paddy Power and Ladbrokes. A more loyal-looking throng huddled around the independent bookies who stood on small plinths. There was excitement about a dog called Wet Declan. I could gather that he was the favourite for the nine fifteen. Starting bets on Gaslight Parsley for the long shot. Six to one, his grandmother was a champion at the Easter Cup. Over-under for Brando's Dartboard. Cash was waved in the air and exchanged for tiny dockets of paper. The wind fluttered the dockets and people pinched them between their fingers. I relished my Benson & Hedges and stood watch like an anthropologist. I texted Brendan and asked him how he was getting on at the cunt of an architect's wedding. 'Shite craic,' he wrote back, 'nobody talking to me, I think they didn't really expect me to come. The vol-au-vents were incredible though. First dance will be starting soon and then I'm robbing pints off tables.' 'Forget them, Brendan,' I texted. 'I'm at the greyhound stadium, it's insane. You have to see these people. Come here and drink with me. It's fifteen minutes in a taxi, I'll pay for it. I'm on my own. Come on.' He wrote back immediately, 'YES' with a laughing emoji.

The initial metallic taste from the Foster's became pleasantly bearable. I huddled with all the punters at the bar for the second pint. We all rubbed off one another. I didn't care, I kind of liked it. A blonde girl pulled the handle of the tap and Foster's slushed into the plastic cup. It stopped halfway and spluttered; beer foam spilled out of the rim all over her hands. 'Number four needs to be changed,' she squealed into the ether. She looked to be twelve years of age. She didn't speak to the customers or make eye contact either. I noticed that all of the bar staff were teenagers or children. The law didn't exist here like it did in the world outside the stadium. The child pulled me a new pint. I took a big gulp. The warm buzz of alcohol made my face feel flush and gave me that comforting hug of drink confidence. Muzzled greyhounds were paraded out in numbered jackets like sick little horses. The oval racing track was smothered in beach sand. A small electric machine drove around it in laps and raked the sand in perfect soft furrows. I wanted someone to care about me the way that machine cared about the sand. It was operated by a man with one arm who looked like Ross Kemp.

Brendan pushed through the greyhound people in his navy outlet store suit and a mismatched tie. All of it was two sizes too small. His thighs fought the seams like he was trudging through deep mud. As he moved towards me, he began shouting. 'What in Christ's name are you doing wearing that big jacket, Pamela?

Is that the one from your office yesterday? You look like you've been in a car accident. You look like a paramedic tried to prevent you from going into shock.' 'Piss off, Brendan, your suit is disgusting,' I retorted. I was thrilled to see Brendan. I quenched my fag out in my drink and fucked it on the ground. I brought both my freezing hands up against the warmth of his jowls and said, 'You've to catch up now because I'm ready for my third pint. Will we do shots?' His eyes lit up and he said, 'If you're paying, Pamela, yes. Let's do shots.'

The only spirit they had at the bar was Jägermeister. More of a liqueur than a spirit. We both did a shot. It was hot and medicinal. We ordered more pints of Foster's. Fags were chain-smoked. We settled ourselves by a white metal fence, away from the rest of the crowd. I could hear the clatter of the first race starting behind us. I didn't care. Brendan began crying, but not real crying, he winced out a crying type of face to try and make himself cry, and he said, 'What if Cecelia was the one, Pamela? What if she was the one? I know we were only together for three months, and I know it was in college, but what if I just handed over the love of my life to that cunt of an architect? What does he have that I don't have? Tell me, Pamela. Be honest, I can take it. Tell me.' 'Fuck her, Brendan, she's a lesbian,' I said. 'She doesn't deserve you. Neither of them do.' 'That's exactly what I was thinking too, Pamela, but I didn't want to sound cocky,' he replied, flicking the flint on my lighter. Brendan drank the end of his Foster's and placed the plastic glass on the fence on its side. He nestled his phone in it so that it served as a crude speaker. He played the song 'Beachball' by Nalin & Kane. We danced with our fingers in the air and smoked. I didn't feel cold any more.

The merriness was creeping up on me at this point, so we went back to the bar for more shots and pints. I didn't want to lose the buzz. Brendan walked ahead. The left leg of his pants was taut around his calf and a yellow sports sock winked with the rhythm of his steps. The ground of the stadium was littered with those white betting dockets from earlier. A boy with a gigantic sweeping brush was pushing them into neat piles. I ran at one of the piles and kicked the dockets into the air and they flitted down over me like confetti. The boy called me a red-headed bitch. The greyhound people's faces were a mismatch of delight and disappointment. Wet Declan had won the first race. Joyful punters collected their cash from the bookie kiosks. A group of men huddled near Wet Declan and his trainer. The dog was steaming in the floodlights with his tongue hanging out. They were on the other side of the track, and they looked like important men, so I walked towards them and said, 'Which one of you is Cyril Tynan?' A tall fella in a long cream raincoat and a moustache stepped forward. He said with a concerned tone, 'I am Cyril Tynan, who is asking may I enquire?' 'My name is Pamela Furlong, I am a solicitor and I represented the late Noel Riordan.' 'Oh Pamela, Miss Furlong. I recognise your name from your letters, it's nice to finally meet you in person. We were terribly sorry to hear about the passing of poor Noel. He was greatly respected in the greyhound community at one point, all things considered,' he said. The other men grumbled in agreement behind him. 'My client Noel Riordan was an innocent man,' I replied. 'And you are very lucky that he is no longer with us. I was prepared to drag your committee through the highest courts in this country. My client had consistently upheld the utmost standards of ethical conduct and commitment to the welfare of greyhounds under his care. We are firmly of the belief that the decision to ban Noel Riordan was made on the basis of unsubstantiated claims and/or an erroneous interpretation of the events in question. It is sadly too late now. But you were wrong, sir. And you and the rest of the Limerick

Greyhound Association committee before me should be ashamed.' I kept repeating the word 'ashamed', four or five times, drawing out the vowels. There was a deathly silence. The men of the committee communicated with each other using their eyes and faces only, cautious of libelous words.

A few greyhound people had gathered around to watch, drawn in by the conflict. I could tell that they were highly impressed by my legal speak. I felt like a barrister at my day in court. A lady in a lilac fascinator hat broke the silence with an affected posh accent over a country brogue and said, 'This one is absolutely steaming drunk, look at the state of her, with the big hair and the stolen jacket. She's no solicitor. What solicitor presents themselves like that?' The crowd agreed, they whispered *hoora hoora houla*. The mood was turning against me. There was another contribution. It was the little blonde child who worked at the bar. She quipped with an adult passive aggression, 'I've had to serve that woman with the jacket all night and there's a stink of sweat off her.' Cyril Tynan smirked quietly at this comment like a moustached ferret and I fully lost the plot. I screamed. 'Ye fucking killed him, ye slithery cunts, ye Bastards. He's dead because of ye. He reared Hanley's Fiasco from a pup, he had a revolver buried in a condom full of grease, and ye'd all be shot dead tonight if God hadn't taken him first. Ye Bastards.' I felt two hands on my shoulders. I half expected it to be security. It was the hands of my brother Brendan. 'Jesus Christ, Pamela, you're making a fucking show of us. Stop. I'll be the one to get my head kicked in, not you.' He dragged me away from the absolute Bastards. Brendan offered to take me home in a taxi. 'No,' I said, 'we'll get two more pints, I'm not shook by that. The committee needed to hear all of that,' I said. Brendan began to whisper in a high pitch, 'You told me yourself that you found the tea bags in the jacket, Pamela. He was guilty, he was dosing the dogs with caffeine.' 'That's not the point, Brendan. That's not the point. You don't understand justice, you don't even have a job, I'm a solicitor. Shut up, you're buying the next round.'

The drink had us starving. We both slobbered on horrendous burgers that were more boiled than fried and the grilled onions splurged out the back end and landed on my shoes every time I took a bite. I imagined how dinnery it all smelled. I didn't care. We settled back by the white fence with our pints and my cigarettes and danced to Neil Diamond on Brendan's phone speaker. The wind had turned to that greasy drizzle and it sparkled like glitter in the floodlights of the stadium. *Hoora hoora houla*. A country voice farted over the tannoy and announced that the last race would begin in fifteen minutes. The voice listed out the dogs who would race. Final bets now. An excitement jumped up through me and I turned to Brendan and said, 'That's Pamela Fags' first race, Brendan. Listen. Pamela Fags. Pamela Fags.' He looked at me like I had twelve arses, but when I explained why there was a greyhound called Pamela Fags, he insisted on placing a bet on her. I didn't think he had any money until he launched into his breast pocket and took out the fifty euro note that he'd found in the multi-storey car park. He'd kept it for good luck, he told me. Brendan rushed over to the red-faced bookies for twelve to one odds on Pamela Fags. When he came back, he said, 'This has fuck all to do with a dog, Pamela. This is me betting on you, because I believe in you. I couldn't be prouder to have you as a little sister. We're all so proud of you and all that you've become, and Daddy would say the exact same if he was here.' He was shit-faced. We hugged furiously and he told me how much I smelled like sweat and burgers.

I hung over the side of the fence, absolutely rat-arsed. I got my first squint at Pamela Fags. She was slender and noble with a sandy coat and a little white triangle on her forehead. Her body was immaculately clean and marbled with tight musculature. Black startled eyeballs. The type of eyes you want on a greyhound. I could tell there was a champion in her yet. She wore a purple jacket with the number four on it. I watched her breath rising up through the wire of her muzzle and I blew smoke out of my nose. We were one and the same. Her handler gently caressed her hind quarters to keep her calm. He wore a white coat like a doctor and I imagined that he was Noel Riordan spinning his teeth around in his mouth. God rest his soul.

The six dogs were led into their traps for the race to commence. Silence came over the crowd until all you could hear was the electrical hum of the mechanical hare being switched on. The dogs were poised like springs in the box. They barked with excitement. 'Number one Gelded Emmet is seven to four joint favourite with Canary Warp. Continental Breakfast in a point at five to four. Eight to one Strokestown Voyager, twenty to two Elvis Has Risen, and the promising new bitch Pamela Fags trained by Dinny Ryan and named by the late Noel Riordan, outsider of the party, Pamela Fags in at twelve to one.' There was a solemn clap from the greyhound people when Noel's name was called out over the stadium, the absolute Bastards.

'The hare comes round the bend and they're off. It's a very level break. Number one Gelded Emmet makes a head start. Strokestown Voyager coming up on the inside. Strokestown Voyager. Elvis Has Risen tracks them on the outside. And it's Elvis Has Risen with his eye on the hare. They've run off the turn there now and down the far side. Number four Pamela Fags emerging from the rear and it's Canary Warp and Continental Breakfast beginning to inch up. Gelded Emmet shows in front and there goes Strokestown Voyager up between them to split, on the inside is Pamela Fags, and these three are a few lengths clear, and it's Elvis Has Risen again, overtaking Pamela Fags from the rear, but it's Strokestown Voyager and Gelded Emmet who are neck and neck racing up towards the finish, Continental Breakfast falls to the back, Pamela Fags is trying hard, Elvis Has Risen, Elvis Has Risen, overtaking Pamela Fags, Canary Warp is rearing to catch up, not looking great for Continental Breakfast but it's a great battle tonight here at Limerick Greyhound Stadium and Strokestown Voyager takes the finish line, a good run there from Gelded Emmet in second, and Elvis Has Risen who managed to snatch third place.'

The whole thing only lasted a minute. The dogs still chased the hare even though the race was over. The mechanical hare disappeared behind a green Paddy Power advert and the hounds all gathered aimlessly beside a breeze-block wall. Pamela Fags jumped and barked at her trainer, staining his white coat with her muddy paws. Her tail wagged in excitement like she wasn't a loser. Steam rose from her muscles and there was a joyful madness in her black eyes. Her pink tongue hung long like luncheon meat and she drooled on the perfectly furrowed sand. She was pathetic. She was disgusting. I hated her. Brendan stood beside me in defeated silence. I watched his fist crush the betting docket in his hand. 'FUCK,' he roared. 'FUCK, FUCK, FUCK.' 'Oh shut up, Brendan, it wasn't even your fifty euro to begin with,' I snarled. Pamela Fags was ushered away on a leash. Off to have her hind quarters caressed and lavished with expensive dog food no doubt. I couldn't look at her any longer. That old familiar pain stabbed at my stomach and I vomited on the concrete. My heaves were hoora hoora houla. I wiped my mouth dry with the sleeve of Noel's tweed jacket. The retching awoke my olfactory senses and a stench of pints and burgers and puke and old man sweat paraded through my nostrils. I turned to Brendan and said, 'If we ring a taxi now, we'll make last orders in Charlie Malone's.' We left the greyhound stadium and Brendan played me Linkin Park in his plastic pint glass.

Covert Japes

'1964 Höfner Violin Bass For Sale. Original, very few in circulation. Full hollow body bass guitar with warm resonant sound, of the kind Paul McCartney played throughout the '60s. Solid maple neck. 22-fret rosewood with dot inlays. Sunburst finish. This vintage gem is equipped with two original Höfner 511B 'Staple' pickups, offering that unmistakable '60s bass sound. Starting offers at 500 euro. I'm not looking to make a fortune, just hoping it goes to someone who'll appreciate it as much as I have. 089 654 3421.'

This was the advert that had me in a shopping centre car park at 7.30 a.m. in the rain, trying my best to get the heater to defog the windows. I was looking out at a bruiser of a morning where the sun is up but the street lights are still on. You could drink the air. All the parking spaces were layered with moss, and a dog in the distance had a cough from barking. Not many cars over on the road. A white RTÉ News van drove past. The estate behind the shopping centre has its problems; there must have been another shooting last night. I rang the number in the advert a few times yesterday but never got an answer. I received a text back with this address. I was told to go to a pub called The Imperial Bar. The Imperial Bar? The Imperial Bar is a pub you only hear about. You wouldn't go in there. It's not dangerous as such, it's just that it's a pub stuck into the backside of the Southside Shopping Centre, which isn't much of a shopping centre. Well, it had been in the '90s, but the recession tore the hole off it. All shuttered up except for a discount store and a place that sells mobility scooters to the elderly.

I wondered if this was a trap. When I shut my car door, I heard the rattle of rust between the panels. My 500 euro would be better spent on a new jalopy. I walked towards the entrance of the pub. The facade was cladded in this Celtic Tiger cream veneer. Fake carved wood all blistered. A Guinness poster in the window with the top half bleached by sun. Who drinks here? Why? Secret alcoholics and accountants having affairs? I stuck my car key out between my fingers just in case. This would be a great way to rob me or murder me, in fairness. Who in the name of Jaysus is selling a 1964 Höfner bass for 500 euro? Those things could go to auction for six grand easy. This has to be a trap. There'll be a load of bowsies with baseball bats inside that pub and I'll deserve whatever happens to me. I'm a right idiot for agreeing to this. I felt an instinct to turn back, but the curiosity had the bateing of me. There was a relief when I saw the security camera pointing down at the door. It had the flashing little red light. At least if something terrible does happen to me, I know that I'm being recorded entering the bar. I fixed my hair when I imagined the footage playing on TV in one of those missing persons shows. I considered turning back once more. Fuck it. I went to knock on the door, but it had been unlatched.

It was dark inside except for the frosty glow of a fridge behind the bar top. The pub wasn't open yet. Harp, Guinness and Bulmers. The Holy Trinity. 'We show Sky Sports' on the wall beside the old TV. OK, not too bad. Upturned chairs resting on wooden tables. The sourness of spilled booze and the cheesy bleach bang of a bad mop. There was the reassuring bite of pine and lemon from a fresh urinal cake too. The place can't be too bad if they're topping up the urinal cakes. 'Hello,' I said into the blackness. A much older man who looked to be in his late fifties emerged from the men's toilets and said pure sprightly, 'Pull across the latch behind you. I'll be with you now in a minute, pick a table for yourself. You'll have a coffee, you will?' 'I will,' I said, 'that'd be lovely.' He was no punter. He had the movements of a person who worked here and was opening early to meet me. He came around from the bar with a cup of milky instant coffee in his right hand and placed it down on my table. 'There you are now.' He walked back up to make his own cup. I sipped the bitter Nescafé and took in his appearance. There was a bit of length to the back of his haircut, the type of deliberate length that lets you know it used to be longer in his youth. Doc Martens shoes under light-blue denim jeans, matching denim shirt, red-wine silk waistcoat and a dainty little silver earring. This was the uniform of a man who'd been playing in bands a long time. Probably does the odd wedding or corporate gig and moonlights in this pub to supplement his income. Flexible hours, never too busy, makes sense. This was definitely a fucker with a bass to sell. I was certain of it. I relaxed. No one was getting their head kicked in this morning.

The man sat down opposite me and raised his coffee up to his lips. He told me his name was Gerry and asked if I'd like to see the bass. 'I would love that, Gerry, have you it close by?' I said. He reached behind with one hand and carefully placed a guitar case across the table. A battered-looking old leather thing pocked with stickers from bands and festivals and destinations. Fender, Ernie Bell, Chris Rea, Van Morrison, Ronnie Scott's, Glastonbury, I Love NY. There was no faking that, the guitar case had earned those stickers. This was legit gear. My heart began to race with the excitement. 'Can I see it?' I asked. 'Hold on to your horses now, lad, I'll only open this case for the right person,' he responded. He said it like a da, with his right palm down on the case, guarding it like a bag of fish supper. He continued, 'As I said in the advert, I'm not looking to make a fortune. I know well how much this can sell for online, but some things are worth more than money. What's important to me here is making sure it goes to the right person.' He'd my jocks down at that point. I got foolish, I started trying to impress him. I lost the run of myself, telling Gerry that I play in wedding bands but that my hope is to move to London and get some session work. I own a Fender Mexican Jazz Bass, but a real Höfner is what will take me to the next level and get me the good jobs. I told him that my style is rooted in the Motown warmth of James Jamerson, blended with the complexity of Victor Wooten, but I also had a deep respect for the simplicity of Paul McCartney's more melodic playing. 'I wouldn't dream of replacing the pickups or anything like that, I'd keep her as she is,' I said. I talked myself up beyond my ability and I'd be fucked if he asked me to demonstrate anything on the instrument. But Gerry wasn't impressed or fazed. He had the way of a man who'd heard this chat too many times. He snapped at me a bit and said, 'Anyone can learn to play the bass, son. What I'm looking for is the person who is spiritually mature enough to own it.' This is when shit started getting weird and I wondered if there was a fucking bass inside that case at all. 'Let me tell you a story about the man who owns this bass,' Gerry said.

'The man who owns this bass nearly had a record deal with EMI in 1983. His band were called Furious Moonlight and they toured two dates with Kajagoogoo in Denmark. There was a six-month period in Limerick city when you couldn't enter a men's toilet without hearing someone say "Furious Moonlight will be the Irish Flock of Seagulls". John Peel almost aired their demo tape on BBC Radio One but the IRA bombed Woolwich that weekend, and that fucked it all. The record labels went cold and the crowds got smaller. It's a cruel ould bollocks of a game, lad. Furious Moonlight fell apart, but the reputation carried enough weight that he got gigs as a stand-in bass player for other bands. A session head. A job he wouldn't wish on a convicted pervert. Touring as a bass player is like a party with no beginning and no end. Which might sound glamorous to a young lad like yourself, but you have to go home to your own bed at some point. Hotel rooms and corridors blurred into a purgatory of roadies and sound engineers. The rush of being up on stage in front of an audience that you haven't earned is as dangerous as any line of chang. It's an artificial buzz that you end up chasing through other means. Before long he was shelving wads of coke up his own winker on tour buses.

'Let me tell you about the man who owns this bass. The man who owns this bass once lit a cigarette for Kate Bush, she held eye contact too, and he would have been in there if he only had the gumption to make the move. He still thinks about it in the red heat of night time. He watched Sting fall head first into a bain-marie of hot stroganoff in the catering tent. He helped Axl Rose find his lost sunglasses backstage at Glastonbury. He toured with The Housemartins, Aztec Camera, Gary Numan, fucking Prefab Sprout. He saw it all. But the lights were too bright. He grew fond of the drink and the dandruff. His rhythm went arseways. He fucked up a couple of gigs for Martin Kemp and was demoted to being the guitar tech. He tuned the bass and kept the strings fresh for another man to live in the spotlight. Always the runner up. He never stood on a stage again but he still chased the rush of it. Touring with the crew and not the band, and he toured until he lost the feeling of having a home.

'Train stations and airports became his home. He could tell you the colour of the carpet in the Luton Airport bar on 19 March 1993. It was purple with yellow squiggles and triangles. And he can tell you that because that's where he had his last drop of the demon drink. He'd been on a seventy-hour Paddy's Day bender while working Jason Donovan's 'Between the Lines' tour. Newcastle Brown Ale it was. He can still taste it now. His sweat was like the condensation on the back of a fridge and it smelled like a bin. Earlier on, he'd wept into a *Woman's Own* in WHSmith. Dangling off the Devil's bell-end he was. The drink, the sleeplessness and the hangover had all mired into one river of misery. He lost himself in the carpet of the Luton Airport bar and decided how he was going to die. He would get on his flight, wait until the plane got a bit of altitude, and open the emergency exit. He'd jump out somewhere between Derby and

Manchester, and bollocks to anyone else who got sucked out with him. A rock star's death. He figured he'd get one last rush from the descent before his corpse penetrated the attic of someone's house.

'When the tannoy called out his flight number, he finished the pint and accepted his destiny. But something glinted at him from beyond the sadness. He saw a sign beside the airport toilets that said "Multi-faith Prayer Room". People of all persuasions walked in and out with a look of peace and contentment on them. "Multi-faith Prayer Room," he said to himself, "I wonder what goes on in there?" Now, the man who owns this bass wasn't religious in any shape or form. But he was definitely pining for the peace and contentment that he saw on those faces. He sensed a force drawing him towards the Multi-faith Prayer Room. It took him away from the airport bar and he walked inside. Heavy on the feet, mind, after all the drink and the coke. He might have done a shart earlier too.

'The Multi-faith Prayer Room was sparse. A beige carpet and a smell of car fresheners. There were no crucifixes or nothing like that. But there was a stained-glass window with a lightbulb behind it. That was it. A neutral space for having a chat with whatever God you wanted. Take your pick. Pure silence, you'd nearly forget that it was an airport. Three other people were in the room, each locked into different forms of prayer. There was a Christian on her knees with her hands out, a Muslim fella bent over a bit of carpet, and a Buddhist meditating with his legs crossed. The man who owns this bass had forgotten how to pray. He didn't even know which God he should be talking to. His body swayed with the drink and his movement distracted the other people from their prayers. They could probably smell him too. The Christian woman opened her eyes and stared at him in judgement. He considered turning and leaving. He began to panic with the ould rotten memory of stage fright. A peace suddenly washed over him though, a sensation of falling back into a powerful set of trusting arms. He received a vision of a bass string wobbling on the fret board. The wobble of the string reminded him of the movements of a maggot. He replicated this movement with his torso, rotating his hips and allowing a pulse to travel up from his feet to his hands. He crawled around the carpet of the Multi-faith Prayer Room in a sequence of rhythmic wriggling thrusts. He moved like he was plucking out a song with his limbs. The timing was odd: it had the 2/4 of a bossa nova but with the quarter note of a beguine. You know what I mean, lad? It lasted for several minutes. He was experiencing divine ecstasy. All the truth of the universe sang in his head. The Muslim, the Christian and the Buddhist stopped their prayers and observed him on the floor in pure reverence and awe. When he'd finished, the Buddhist kneeled down and asked him which religion he belonged to and what prayer or ritual he'd just partaken in. The man who owns this bass didn't know where these words came from, but his mouth started moving regardless. He told the Buddhist that he worshipped The Maggot.

'The three stood looking with their jaws open, waiting for him to tell them more. He began to ask all three to describe Heaven. They each told an account of a beautiful open place filled with sunlight, trees and birdsong. "Sounds gorgeous," he said. So he asked them to describe Hell. They all spoke of punishment, death and decay. "I don't like the sound of that place," he replied. They did those superior religious chuckles, like you'd hear at an AA meeting. He got up from the floor and paced back and forth, feeling the confidence that a lead singer would have. Then he asked them, "What would Heaven look like to a maggot?" They had no answer to this. He repeated it, "Somebody here tell me what Heaven would look like to a maggot."

No response again. He reported back to them gently that they had all described a vision of Heaven that was perfectly tuned to the needs of human life. Sunlight, birds and open spaces. But to a maggot, that eternity would be a vision of Hell, because maggots experience their vitality in the darkness and rot of corpses. If you could ask a maggot what its idea of eternal bliss is, it would describe a land littered with cadavers and decay. A maggot's Heaven is a human's vision of Hell and a human's Heaven is a maggot's vision of Hell. "So somebody has it wrong," he said, "and I reckon it's us humans. We have created a selfish bastard vision of Heaven and that's why maggots show up when we die. They're not eating us; the maggots are informing our corpses that we got it all wrong. But by the time we're silent enough to listen, it's too late. So that's why I worship The Maggot."

'The three onlookers asked him how long he had worshipped The Maggot. He was honest. He informed them that they had just witnessed the one true religion being revealed to him by God. The Muslim, the Christian and the Buddhist immediately dropped to their knees. They begged to become his disciples. He accepted them as his disciples. They all wriggled like maggots on the floor of the Multi-faith Prayer Room and out over the tiles of Luton Airport past the gift shop. He missed his flight to Glasgow. Jason Donovan could get fucked at this point.

'His disciples asked him why The Maggot was worthy of their worship. He told them that it's because no life on Earth can escape The Maggot. You could be Axl Rose, Kate Bush or Martin Kemp and The Maggot would still visit your body when you die. Maggots don't care about record deals or whether John Peel played your demo tapes. Jason Donovan is equal to a dead rat in the eyes of The Maggot. But if you can submit to the inevitability of the Maggot's mouth, you will know true humility in life. He wasn't even sure what that meant, but it made sense to him and his disciples agreed. He added that maggots move in the shape of a sine wave. He used his finger to draw a wriggly sine wave in the air. The sine wave is the shape that a perfect bass note makes when it moves through the room. Musical mathematics is the language of God because it transcends the limits of words and is understood universally by our bodies. Music is the maggots of the air. The ex-Muslim agreed with this. They got up off the floor and sat at the airport cafe and drank those gigantic 1990s cappuccinos that were all foam and no coffee. He explained to his disciples that there were three stages to a maggot's lifecycle: the egg, the pupa and the fly. What they had all witnessed in the Multi-faith Prayer Room was him wriggling out of his pupae stage and transcending into the fly stage. The ex-Buddhist was pleased with that explanation. The ex-Christian was sceptical. She asked what their sacrament would be. He reached into his pocket and pulled out a guitar plectrum, held it with both hands and swallowed it. "There's your sacrament," he said. The ex-Christian fell to her knees and worshipped his Doc Martens, renouncing Christ in that very moment.

'His disciples asked him how they could all transcend their pupae stage and become flies. He told them that they would need to save humanity by teaching as many people as possible about this new religion. "We should buy four tickets on the next flight out of Luton Airport," he instructed. It was a flight to Mykonos. The ex-Christian paid for it, she was a minted Yank. And so he and his disciples boarded the plane.

'The plan was to hijack the plane by taking control of the intercom. This was the gig that would make or break them. They would use the intercom to explain the urgency of The Maggot to the other passengers. Then he would open the emergency exit and all four of them would sacrifice themselves to the wind. But they wouldn't fall to their deaths. Instead, divine intervention would cause translucent wings to grow from their backs. They would then buzz around the airplane and wave at all the passengers inside. Every passenger on the plane will have witnessed a miracle. The plane will land safely. By the next morning, the miracle will be reported by every newspaper in the world. It was a solid fucking plan, lad, and his disciples were sold on it.

'The plan went tits up, of course. About eight minutes into the flight, the man who owns this bass rushed for the emergency exit and pressed down on the red lever that manually opens the door. It swung out violently. The wind was something shocking, but the cabin hadn't been pressurised yet, so no one got sucked out. It was just awful loud and windy. He tried his best to tell the passengers about his religious beliefs, but nobody could hear a word and they were all screaming too. He got stage fright. It wasn't working out the way he'd planned in his head, so he jumped and regretted it immediately. His left hand grabbed the plane door. He was dangling outside the fucking airplane, holding on until his fingers went white. He didn't dare look down. His disciples chickened out.

Within seconds the ex-Buddhist and an air hostess crunched the door shut on his left hand. This actually saved him from falling to his death. But he stayed hanging from the outside like Hitler's bollock. It wasn't painful; pain isn't too much of a concern when you're in a situation like that. Then the wind picked up; stuck him to the fuselage like a fly on a swatter. In and out of consciousness. The plane turned around and made an emergency landing back at Luton Airport within six minutes. Fair play to the pilot. A fire crew and ambulance were waiting on the runway. The paramedics could not believe that he had survived the ordeal. A miracle they called it. It made the papers all right, but not one of the dirty rags reported on his message or his spiritual revelation. The other passengers only heard the accent, and the IRA got all the credit again. Of course, he spent the next year in hospital with broken ribs and one side of him in bits. His left hand was mangled by the plane door and it had to be amputated at the wrist.'

My eyes darted around The Imperial Bar, searching for a hidden camera. Gerry recounted the entire story with a straight face in one take. He'd definitely told it a few times before. But if he was an actor, he was a bloody good one. My instinct now was that this was a prank. Maybe one of the lads had set me up and planted that advert in the newspaper, knowing well I couldn't resist a 500 euro Höfner bass. Before I could even open my mouth with a response, Gerry brought his left hand up and slammed it down on the guitar case. The hand was peach in colour and made crudely out of rubber. It was solid and heavy, like a hand you'd buy in a joke shop. His middle finger bent at an angle around his wedding band. 'Now lad, you can see why I'm selling this bass,' he said. 'There's two things I haven't done for the past thirty years: I haven't had a drop of the demon drink, and I haven't played the bass.' 'Do you mind if I use the jax, Gerry?' I said. 'Over beyond to the right of the bar,' he said.

I targeted my stream of piss at the urinal cake. I pushed with force and budged it from left to right. It gave me a feeling of control over my thoughts. My piss was yellow and I watched it swirl green down the drain when it hit the blue cake. The fresh smell of toilet pine rose up at me. I wasn't thinking about the bass, I was thinking about The Maggot. Because the Maggot religion made a lot of sense to me. I wondered if I had been chosen by a higher power. I considered getting down on to the tiles of the jax and wriggling out towards Gerry in pure devotion. I snapped out of that delusion fairly quickly, because who in the fuck goes to The Imperial Bar at eight in the morning and comes out joining a new religion? Not me. I walked back out to Gerry and sat down.

'We need to start chatting about the bass now, Gerry, because the traffic will get wicked in about twenty minutes. But I do have one question that's killing me. What happened to your disciples?'

'I did a stint of rehab after hospital, spent a year in a wheelchair. I questioned everything that happened in that Multi-faith Prayer Room. You can't trust an episode like that after a decent bender. I was interrogated relentlessly by English police, of course. MI5 too. Asking about my politics. They lost interest when I kept bringing up The Maggot though. As for the disciples, they visited me one by one over the years that followed. They hadn't stayed in contact with each other. I got a sense that they were embarrassed by it all. Embarrassed to have allowed themselves to be overcome by the ecstasy of it. The Christian told me that it had felt like a one-night stand that she regretted. They had all returned to their respective religions too. But what brought them back to visit me was a respect for my faith, the fact that I'd actually gone ahead with the plan. Each of them tried to convert me over to their religions, but I refused. "I'm sticking with The Maggot," I told them.'

There was a sincerity in how quickly Gerry answered my question. It threw me off. His eyes had a truth in them. 'So you've no disciples any more then, Gerry?' I asked him. 'Well, that's what brings us here, son. I'm a one-man religion. Solo like Martin Kemp. The man who will own this bass must carry the message of The Maggot forward to the people. The man who's going to own this bass must prove his spiritual maturity to me. And you're the first person to make it this far in the test.' Gerry then used his good hand and clacked the latches on the guitar case. He pushed open the cover. There she was, smiling up at me. A 1964 Höfner violin bass. Shining like it was hanging from Paul McCartney's shoulder. Sunburst finish, solid maple neck. 22-fret rosewood with dot inlays and original Höfner 511B 'Staple' pickups. This was the real deal. My mouth went dry with desire. But as Gerry lifted the neck with his right hand, he stroked the body with his left hand. His rubber fingers made a squeaking sound against the varnish and they bent at the tips. The big ridiculous peach hand poked out of his denim shirt. It just didn't look like an actual medical pros-thetic. It was a joke shop hand. It did not convince me. I became very sceptical. Somebody was having me on here, but I was hungry for that bass.

Gerry took a big swig of his Nescafé and said, 'Forget the money, lad. I'll give you this Höfner for free if you become the next disciple of The Maggot.' He made the shape of a sine wave in the air with his rubber finger and told me that real bass playing happens in the soul and not in the hands. I felt a hint of fear gripping me and I asked him, 'And how exactly do I become a disciple of The Maggot, Gerry?' A bit of a mad look arrived in his eyes, and he goes, 'Abstinence and sacrifice, son. The man who inherits this bass can own it, but he can never play it. I have a butcher's block behind the bar, and a sterilised cleaver. I'll do it in one swipe, just below the wrist. We'll ring an ambulance in advance, and they'll have painkillers and all that. With a clean wound you'd be right in two weeks. Then we'll bury the hand under an oak tree and let the maggots purify the flesh.' I didn't fully take in the severity of what he'd just asked of me and I responded instantly, 'But Gerry, if I've only one hand then I can't play the bass, even if it's mine to play.' 'And now you understand the pure truth of existence. You're definitely the right man for this,' he said. 'Give me a moment to think about this please, Gerry,' I replied.

'Take your time, I've some bits to do behind the bar. I'll come back in a few minutes. There's no pressure here, this is a big decision, lad. You're free to walk if you like.'

I leaned back in the chair and started doing some serious detective work in the silence of my own head. Columbo shit. I put a few pieces together and began to figure out exactly what was happening here. Last night, when I enquired about the advert for the bass guitar, that TV programme *Covert Japes* was playing in the background of my apartment. It's the hidden camera show that's on RTÉ2, the fella with the quiff presents it. It's not for me, but it's a good laugh if you're a fucking idiot. They travel all around Ireland and get actors to prank members of the public by placing them in ridiculous situations. They dress up as traffic wardens or pretend that an alien invasion is happening. That type of shite. Then, at the end, just when the mark is about to lose their rag, the TV crew jump out and reveal that it's all a big joke. 'Smile for the camera, you've just been Covertly Japed,' they say. The lights turn on, hugs and laughs, lots of clapping. The member of the public always wins a prize too. Then the credits roll down the screen, hahahaa. Here's my evidence. Firstly, Gerry is clearly an actor wearing a costume.

His story about his band and the prayer room is too far-fetched to be true. Hanging off the side of a moving airplane? That didn't happen. He delivered it to me in one straight take, like a script that he had rehearsed. Then, the way he revealed his fake hand at the end felt perfectly timed for laughs. There was probably a camera zoomed in on my face for my reaction to that. Secondly, who drinks in The Imperial Bar? Fucking nobody drinks in The Imperial Bar, it's always empty. Because it's a pub at the side of a dead shopping centre. Last summer, I did a temp job as a runner for a TV company after the pandemic shut down all the live music. I hated it, but I did learn a thing or two about making TV. The Imperial Bar is exactly the type of place that is quiet enough and cheap enough for an RTÉ crew to hire out and film in for the day. Also, TV shoots start very early. So that's why we're here at eight in the morning. Aaaaand, that's why I saw the white RTÉ van drive past on the road earlier. They're obviously down from Dublin for this. Thirdly, his fucking hand. It's a joke shop rubber hand. If he actually lost his hand, then he'd have a convincing medical prosthetic, not that peach yoke that sounds like a dildo when he slaps it on the table. That's the silly prop, the 'hero prop' they call it in TV language. Its purpose is to make me look like a big eejit on telly if I believe that it's real. This whole pub is obviously rigged with TV cameras, but they've done an amazing job at hiding them. That is what is happening here. It's all coming into place now. If I play along, the crew will jump out, hugs and smiles, and then they'll present me with that vintage '64 Höfner as the prize. Boom. Not a bad result for a Tuesday morning.

I got into character and said to Gerry, 'I'm ready to become a disciple, Gerry. The revelation you had in the Luton Airport prayer room has convinced me to worship The Maggot. I'm not afraid.' The actor who played Gerry couldn't believe his luck. He was beaming. 'Are you sure about this? There's no going back, son.' 'I've never been more certain about anything before in my life, Gerry,' I responded.

He walked me up towards the bar and said, 'Could you give me some help lifting the butcher's block, it's a two-hand job?' That line was clearly written into the script as a sex pun. 'Take it easy, Gerry. I'm here to buy a bass, not to get a wank.' They'd probably beep that out but I couldn't resist. I lifted the butcher's block up and laid it across the bar top. It was heavy. Gerry reached for the old landline on the wall and dialled 999 with his rubber finger and said, 'I need an ambulance at The Imperial Bar, Southside Shopping Centre. There's been a very serious workplace accident. Please come quickly, he's bleeding heavily.' The phone probably wasn't even connected. I made a face like I was terrified. I'm a natural performer, so I chattered my teeth too. I could hear the canned laughter in my head when the camera cuts to my face. If I do a good enough job of this, who knows, I could get booked to play a few more weddings. RTÉ is decent exposure, like. Gerry started laying down tea towels on the floor underneath the bar. 'No point in making a mess,' he said. I opened my mouth really wide in shock and bulged my eyes out, playing up my reactions for the camera. He took out the cleaver and grabbed it in his right hand. From where I was standing, it looked like an actual butcher's cleaver rather than a fake prop. This meant that the crew would all jump out for the big reveal just before he pretended to bring it down on my hand. 'When you're ready, roll up the sleeve of your left arm and place it down there on the block. Grab a hold of the bar top to steady yourself with your other hand too. I'll have time to move behind you if you faint. A head injury isn't part of the bargain.' I did as he asked, and I practised a look of surprise in my head. There was one detail that niggled at me though. *Covert Japes* wasn't the type of TV show that had a six-grand Höfner violin bass in the budget. It didn't seem like a prize they'd give away. The prizes were usually gift vouchers or a weekend at a spa in Wicklow. Gerry raised the cleaver high above his right shoulder and I held out my wrist.

Rat Lungworm

Joop Houlihan had been a fancy man to the women of Thurles in his time. They went arseways for his Greek squint and the streak of Kevin Costner's jaw under his teeth. He'd a wardrobe pregnant with Ben Sherman shirts that glistened like a packet of fruit pastilles. Every weekend he'd pick a new colour and drape it over his shoulders, his television presenter shoulders. A hungry head of hair for eating tubs of Brylcreem.

Above in Coco's Paradise. The local disco on a small stretch of floorboards atop a bar and grill. It's an Aldi now but it was a temple of sound back then. It had a tropical theme in the time of line dancing. The fingers of Thurles reaching through the pink flashing cloud of a fog machine to touch the tribal tattoo on Joop's tricep once the shirt came off. He was the Child of Prague on a horn. Arms like the Guards wouldn't dig out of a Shinner's back garden. His arse too. None of this gym shit. Pumped up from when they used to pay a tenner a brick on the building sites. A Jack Russell's arse, fighting to get out of the stonewashed 501s. The women of Thurles would rest their Bacardi Breezers on it.

And fuck me could he line dance. Didn't matter what the DJ threw at him, could be Garth Brooks, could be Gigi D'Agostino. He had his own way of line dancing, a flamenco flair. A cowboy on a beach he was. Doing a sailor step shuffle on stabby patent toes that could burst a balloon just by tipping off the gossamer of it. Shirt floorwards and a Bruce Willis vest with crystals of odourless sweat giving him big red fireplace nipples. Effortless pull-ups on the fire exit so you'd see the fur of his Europop oxters. Topless and shining. The din of Lynx, Tabac on the bollox. No selfies, your head was the camera back then.

Famished gants dripping from here to Benbulbin and back in a devil's echo. Other men would hide behind the car park bins, breastfeeding their pints, just to watch him barnacle the women of Thurles buckled on the bonnet of his Toyota Celica. And now look at him. Over in the cul-de-sac, a terror to the slugs with salt.

Heineken and kebabs hadn't been kind to Joop in the twenty odd years that followed. He rode the back off the Celtic Tiger, but the recession had the bateing of him. He'd glared into too many blue sparks from a welder's torch and his eyesight wasn't the best. His chubby heart would flutter at a flock of seagulls slicing through the moonlight that he mistook for a meteor shower. Panging for a hot orange rock of luck. There'd been money in laying bricks and he even swung a jab at being a property developer, but lost it all to a time-share in Belarus. Scammed by a plastic-chinned economist from RTÉ.

No family to speak of. Joop had never landed a solid woman and he was in his fuck looking for one now. Sure why would anyone take him in this state? And wouldn't the rejection be a disrespect to his younger self? Wouldn't it be better to exist as a memory in their heads? At least he had held on to the pebbledash bungalow in the cul-de-sac. But it was forever condemned to be a bachelor's hole. You couldn't draw in a woman with an uninsulated crawl space attic. The mania of a tall hedge and ivy sucking all the light from the windows. A woman could walk across his cul-de-sac and never know it was there. Joop was tucked away under a brick in the dark, only crawling out for the shopping and Tuesday's dole. He stuck himself to the walls of the bungalow. They knew more about him than he knew about himself. He had become invisible.

The ivy brought wildlife after the rain. Himself and the long olive slugs of the back porch. Oozing up from the dirt in their hundreds and laying disco-light trails across the decking. On nights of Heineken he was King of the Slugs. Seldom and Gomorrah. They were devoted to him.

'Ye can have the lager or ye can have the salt,' he'd splutter.

And they'd fizzle or fatten depending on his mood. Big Hieronymus Bosch head on him. They were fucked either way. In their hour of judgement, he'd wash the slithery cunts away with a roar of ochre piss from his manhood. Chomping bites at the teal steam of his voice darting up in the dark. Taking gullible words back.

And if the whiskey from Aldi was involved, well he might pick up a slug and slide it down his tongue, then imagine himself as a fuchsia-shirted property developer, perched on the stool of an oyster bar in Heathrow Airport lounge. Laughing with the pebbledash gable wall like it was an oil sheikh on a flight to Riyadh. This life that had been nearly in his fists.

Directing torrents of fizzy champagne piss up

towards his lips. Splashing it on himself. Despising himself. Sure who'd be looking? Slugs are the oysters of the porch when your eyes are gammy with whiskey on board. And then would come the line dancing in the warmth of the bungalow. The phone sat in a teacup. Reverberating Garth Brooks through the kitchen, crooning over the gas hob, while Joop's withering kneecaps did their best through denim on the lino. And fifty-minute floppy wanks to the Celica bonnet lickouts in the car park of Coco's Paradise before he lost himself to the inevitable suffering of existence. With a Peperami of a langer and a manky snooze in the acrylic recliner, he laid bricks in his dreams, and all the slugs were gone by dawn. Back into the concrete like slimy faeries.

The next morning he'd suck a Silk Cut and stare at their pearly trails and his head would be transported back to the kebab boxes that littered car parks on the Sunday after a serious night on the dancefloor. He'd take that over this in a pulse.

The sun didn't spoof at this hour. It let him know that his tribal tattoo was melting green around a sprawl of lavender veins. And they don't really sell Joop any more and these new fucking aftershaves smell like a grapefruit's fanny. The music they have today is the aborted heartbeat of his unborn child – you couldn't line dance to it if you tried.

According to Dr Kiely with the bacon and cabbage face, the slugs were how he contracted rat lungworm disease. *Angiostrongylus cantonensis.* A desperately rare affliction.

The doctor had to drag the information out of him. Asking mad intrusive questions like, 'have you visited the tropics at any point? The Polynesian archipelagos, or Hawaii at all?' and 'have you had any reason to drink rainwater Mr Houlihan, have you consumed unwashed lettuce maybe? This is very important for your prognosis Mr Houlihan, I need to know if you have ever, intentionally or unintentionally, eaten a live slug?'

Joop lied and said he was forced to eat a slug by the Continuity IRA who hunted him down after he caught them raping a postman. The doctor made a face. Joop was fond of a good lie. Like being best friends with Pat Kenny. Or being born in Portugal. Or finding a dog collar that can turn their barks into words. You'd take his stories with a lick of salt. But this story was different, this one was real. He practised it to the gable wall so that it wouldn't sound like one of his lies. 'There's a parasite. An exclusive tropical parasite,' he'd say. 'A rat lungworm they call it – you get it from slugs. The rat gets the worm from eating a slug, and the infected rat passes the worm in his droppings, and a slug eats those droppings so the parasite is in a new slug, which is eaten by another rat. And it goes on and on and on like that for ever. Until a human disturbs the cycle. And I won't tell you how I disturbed that cycle, but now the rat lungworm is inside me and it's travelling up towards the lining of my brain ... There's no cure for it. It's too rare, too special.'

He'd always thought it would be the whiskey in the recliner that would kill him in the end.

But the truth of it was, he had a quare excitement about the rat lungworm. God was shining a torch into his shit eyes. It was the most interesting thing to happen to him since the nineties.

It was a movie star's malady. Type of disease Keanu Reeves would get. Joop's favourite film was *Speed* – he'd watch it on tape and feel the blood hot in his throat over the mad bus with a bomb that would blow up if the bus ever slowed down. And he worshipped the ankles off Sandra Bullock.

He'd see himself and Sandra eating watery oysters in the departure lounge of Heathrow Airport. She'd run her fingernails through his full head of hair, and they'd laugh about getting oyster juice in his curls. Back on the porch, the oyster was a slug and Sandra Bullock was the moon.

And now he felt like the bus in *Speed*, and the rat lungworm was the time bomb, ready to blow his head open if he ever slowed down. And sweet mother of fuck was he lonely in the cul-de-sac. But the rat lungworm climbed into his heart for a while and made it beat faster.

He named the worm Vincent Melrose, which was what he'd want to be named if he hadn't been christened Séamus Houlihan. Joop didn't stop eating the slugs either, he'd wither them with salt and let them sparkle to death in his jowls.

And the glamour of the disease restored a strain of confidence that stretched above the back porch. Over the bony alleys and ghost estates as far as Borrisnoe Mountain. He began to venture beyond the bungalow and slither up into the bowels of Thurles town. He'd developed a way of walking which wasn't quite walking and wasn't quite line dancing, but an agreement between the two.

The worm told him to put on his old Ben Sherman shirts, even with the belly roaring to get out from under the buttons. Stonewashed 501s having a nervous breakdown around his crotch. The muffin-top love handles blushing pink against the Tipperary wind and Brylcreem sliding through his silver hairs. A man who knew what he wanted for breakfast.

And off to the car park of the Aldi he'd go, and say to anyone who'd listen: 'Did you know this place used to be Coco's Paradise? I've a worm in my head that will kill me.'

He expected surprise, to be treated as an exotic novelty, an expensive parrot, someone who'd inspire a distant adoration but instead, he got pity.

'Oh you poor man, Jaysus Joop, if there's anything you need, let me know,' they'd say.

And Thurles town was humming with stories of poor Joop Houlihan above in the cul-de-sac with the parasite.

An online donation page was launched on Joop's behalf by Dickie Herlihy, the Hyundai salesman on the Dublin Road. A fiver here and fifty euro there. The memories of Joop commanding the dancefloor in the days of Coco's Paradise was enough to stir a nostalgic generosity in the middle-aged hearts of Thurles. The bones of eight thousand euro was raised. The cheque flew in the letter box of the bungalow one morning. A warm bubble of gratitude fought to expand in his belly but then he felt embarrassed or belittled or ashamed, and Dickie Herlihy was only a show-off with his Hyundai dealership, and Joop remembers like it was yesterday when Dickie would go red in the face talking to women and copying his dance moves with a tiny priest's arse under the Wranglers. Joop hated every single person who donated that money and he hated himself even more for needing it.

Madeira cakes were left at his door. Mass cards dedicated to St Vitus. He hadn't seen this much attention since 1996. And the women of Thurles were back at the porch like the slugs. Women with haircuts and slabs of husbands. Neasa, Noreen, Maude Cleary, Julia Feeney, Agnes Bourke. Women who'd known the cherry-coloured bonnet of his Toyota Celica, who had shouted, 'come inside me Joop, go harder, drive right into the back where the sticky buns are,' in the time when condoms were for Protestants, long before husbands or haircuts. Sure he couldn't bring that up now.

Even Mary Crawford visited his door, a regular fling from Coco's, a bit more than a fling really – he'd have nearly called her a girlfriend – and she still had the delicate neck but the eyes that were once bowld like a cat's now had a concern in them.

She talked with her teeth and said, 'Is it growing inside you, Joop? Is it really in your brain?'

He avoided the question and said, 'I was cursed with the blonde hair Mary, it always thins on you,' half expecting a compliment.

Mary looked up at his sweating scalp on top of a squint and noticed the sour smell of yesterday's drink on his breath, then changed the subject: 'Are you still at the line dancing, Séamus?'

Joop puffed back his shoulders, sucked in the gut and gave her a wink.

'Ah now Mary, you wouldn't have brought that up if you didn't remember. Line dancing is the vertical expression of a horizontal desire. Come in past the hallway and we'll grapevine and pivot to a bit of Billy Ray Cyrus.'

Mary took a step back and her eyes scanned over the ivy that was eating the bungalow.

'I don't know why I'm here to be honest, Séamus. I wouldn't say that I care about you. I wouldn't say you even enter my head for that matter. But I took that ferry to Liverpool. And you're the only person who knows that. My husband doesn't know. And I think about that. I think about it every single day. And I suppose, I'm never free of you because of it. And I felt some obligation to check in now that you're sick. This isn't about you, or even me. I'm doing it for someone else.'

Joop made a face that let Mary know that he had forgotten all about that business, because it wasn't very important to him.

He closed the door on her and found himself in the hallway and said to nobody: 'Three o'clock is hardly too early for a Heineken, is it?'

And soon he was planted on the back porch langers with 'Cotton Eye Joe' farting out of a tinny phone speaker at twice the BPM of a human heartbeat. The Ben Sherman buttoned wrong, duck-arsing a Silk Cut Purple. Pretending it wasn't Baltic with the east wind. Pretending it wasn't too far gone.

He shuffled and pivoted to the beat, thumb in the denim pocket, spine erect, as good as he ever did it. And the Heineken splashed on the wooden decking like rain and woke up the slugs from the earth and the bricks. Drooling towards the boozy smell of the hops and the yeast and the sugar for their supper. Adoring him, needing him, wanting him. From above, their trails looked like the striations of an anus and Joop was the hole, line dancing and choking on fags.

'Where did you come from, where did you go, which one of ye gets the salt-eyed Joe?' Joop sang to the poor ould slugs.

He was the centre of attention again as he plucked one up and dazzled its neck with a shake of salt from the cellar he kept on the windowsill. The slug dissolved in his fingers and hissed innards from the leather of its khaki skin. It slushed in his mouth all electric and viscous.

The slug was an oyster now, and Joop's head was in Heathrow Airport lounge with the oil sheikh and Sandra Bullock. He'd just flogged a block of apartments to a gobshite in Torremolinos, and was negotiating his tongue around Sandra's mouth. There was talk of a quick fuck in the disabled toilet. There was the cheesy apple waft of an open bottle of Moët on ice and howls of laughter. They were flying somewhere with a white beach that would take the eyes out of your head. He felt the piercing yearn for motherly warmth, wrapped in the curious expressions of the airport peasants. Devouring this radiant and successful man.

But now young Mary Crawford was there with red eyes. She didn't belong here. And her visible sadness was wrecking his buzz. And it stopped being Heathrow

Airport lounge and became a concrete ferry terminal in Rosslare full of vending machines. And suddenly it wasn't an oyster, it was just a fucking slug in his mouth, and it was giving him the gawks and he said to himself: 'Jesus Christ, there's a parasite in my body and it's travelling up towards my brain and it will kill me.'

And he says to Vincent Melrose, the rat lungworm, 'I would have called the child Vincent you know, regardless of gender.'

Joop heard Vincent Melrose say, 'Man up, you fucking arsewipe. That's my name now. Shut up about it.'

And there was no appetite any more for Heinekens or Silk Cuts or oysters of the back porch. No amount of Billy Ray Cyrus could soothe him of the dread that was rising cold on his palms. He wobbled to the kitchen. The harsh fluorescent rod of a ceiling light was turned on. It woke a woodlouse trapped in the plastic of it and projected it on the walls, the size of a German Shepherd.

Joop caught sight of his own reflection in the window. The ashen jawline and sinking eyes like the pockets of a pool table. He tore off the Ben Sherman shirt and let the kitchen see his skin. It was cold.

'I'm a man drowning and waving his arms,' he said to himself.

He waved his hands above his head and took in the wind of his armpits. He splashed on a palmful of Joop aftershave and rubbed it in. Magnolia sandalwood and onions wafted through the bungalow.

He reached for the mobile to call the office of Dr Kiely with the bacon and cabbage face. As the tone rang, he wished he'd have listened to the doctor's words rather than trying to impress him with the lies he'd pulled out of his arse about the IRA. But it was late evening now and the doctor's clinic had no answer. His bowels tourniqueted.

So he took to Google on the old beige monitor in the parlour to learn about the parasite that was growing inside him now. The grandmother carpet. Bare chest in the chair with a blue panic illuminating his flesh. He read about the illness that will take him.

'Severe headaches', 'neck stiffness and fatigue', 'vomiting', 'unusual sensations in the skin, such as tickling, tenderness or burning', 'paralysis', 'coma', 'seizures'. The list of symptoms swung into the front of his head like a soft pink hammer.

'The human is a dead-end host for the rat lung-worm. It can't reproduce inside us, it has nowhere to go, and so it journeys to the meninges of the human brain to die.'

Joop thought of his skull as a graveyard and felt the grope of an anxiety attack. He saw what was ahead of him. Waking up one freezing morning, paralysed in the acrylic recliner. No movement or ability to scream for help. A fixed stare at a greasy gas range, waiting for death by dehydration. Joop knew for certain that he would die alone in the bungalow some time over the next few months. And he cursed the slugs of the back porch. And he cursed Mary Crawford for bringing all of that back at this hour of his life. What good was there in reminding him of that? Ferries and tears and tough decisions. What was the point of that type of thing?

Winter slimed into spring. The worm crept up his spine. Sandra Bullock went to heaven. A slug hadn't been entertained in the bungalow on the porch since the day Mary Crawford called. And there were sudden jumps of the heart in the silence of night time. A fright that might be a cousin of guilt. Notions of contacting her. To finish the conversation she tried to start on the front porch. The whole procedure must have meant an awful lot more to her than it did to him if she needed to speak about it at this stage. It happened so long ago. Maybe he should listen to her experience of it all?

But when Joop travelled inside himself with questions like that and had to root around the Séamus of him, he'd feel a ferocious repulsion. He'd find a person very deserving of rejection and punishment and disgusting things. He had separated from himself at some point in his childhood. He sensed that he was born with a feeling of love, but it had dried up or shut off. He couldn't remember. It was as if the very essence of his Séamusness needed to be concealed with a sweeter smell. He was in no way comfortable in this interior world. The sheets of his bed knew him better than he knew himself.

And before anything resembling a feeling of sadness or self-compassion could rise, he'd become angry with the person who had caused this journey of introspection. And so, he'd lie awake until the room was glowing, and Mary Crawford was only a little slut who shouldn't have let him ride her without a condom in the first place. And didn't he give her the money at the time to go to Liverpool to get it done? And hasn't it been made legal since? And isn't she doing grand for herself now, with a husband and children of her own, while poor Joop has nobody only a parasite climbing up into his brain? So fuck Mary Crawford and her memories.

253

On those mornings he'd hunch at the beige Dell monitor in the parlour. Like a bird, dipping his beak in the fifth mug of Nescafé, with two eyes hanging out of his sockets from tiredness. He'd read the comments in a rat lungworm support group on Facebook and experience a sense of belonging to someone or something. The rarity of the disease meant that the Facebook group was small, just a few hundred accounts. It was a haven for the afflicted and bewildered. Due to the humidity, Hawaii was ideal for the growth and reproduction of the slugs and rats that serve as hosts for the rat lungworm parasite. The majority of the group members resided on the Hawaiian Islands. The page was a place for outpourings of support, camaraderie, links to updates on treatment and pleas for a wider understanding of the disease. This was a community who didn't feel heard or noticed.

Joop could never tell if he was experiencing the symptoms or if he was only imagining them. The years of drink had his bones sore and his skin prickling. He would post in the mornings under the name Vinny Melrose, and soon grew popular in the group because he was from Ireland. Rat lungworm was rare in Europe, but not unthinkable due to the warming climate. He enjoyed being Vinny Melrose on the Facebook group.

Vinny Melrose had no reason to think about Mary Crawford and her abortion. With regular posts, he attained a familiarity with some of the group members. In particular, Skye Reilly from Oahu, a divorced woman of forty-two whose ten-year-old son Aaron was infected with the parasite.

Skye began to message Joop. She was a believer in alternative therapies. She had always yearned to visit Ireland, as her grandfather had come from Kerry. She found herself drawn to this Vinny Melrose character. Skye told him of the great expenses she endured with no insurance under the American health system. Her little son Aaron required regular pain medication and steroid injections for the inflammation since the para- site had entered his nervous system. Joop felt a tender- ness towards Skye, a sudden and overfamiliar affection. A fantastic obsession that he understood to be love. But it was more of a deep need for connection with himself that he would shine on a person like a torch and call it love.

He began to click on her profile several times a day and pore over the little details of her life. He would like all of her comments. He followed the page of the hibachi restaurant where she worked in Pearl City, Oahu. Left an anonymous review praising her table service and friendly manner. He ranked her male friends and arranged them into threat levels in his mind. Skye's ex-husband was a biker, and Joop imagined sending the Continuity IRA to stab him. He wept over the photos of Aaron before the rat lungworm destroyed his young life. He wept over the newer ones where Aaron had a translucent head like a gasping goldfish, with rings under his eyes that carried an adult sadness. There was one photograph of Skye and Aaron in their small apartment, with a white tropical beach visible in the distant background. Skye had strawberry blonde hair and one of those faces that looked like she'd been told two conflicting pieces of information, but Joop's eyes could make her look like Sandra Bullock with the right squint.

She wore wooden beads as jewellery and, in another photo, he saw a feather dreamcatcher hanging in her kitchen. Sometimes she posted about an amethyst crystal that she needed to keep inside a lead jewellery box, because of its power to influence events in her life.

Joop would fantasise about solving all of her problems. He would imagine providing for her and saving her son's life. Marrying her on an ivory beach under a pink sunset in matching linen with those Hawaiian garlands that they have. Oysters on ice with Moët. Line dancing on the sand, while her friends and family envied her and fixated on him. The waves curdling and clacking the round pebbles of the shore. Like something out of an advert for life insurance.

Joop and Skye would message every day now, not just to talk about rat lungworm disease. Conversation turned to more delicate things: favourite foods, travel, interests. He would ask her if she remembered line dancing, and she said that she would have been about twelve when it was popular and that it really wasn't that big of a thing in Hawaii, but she used to love the Backstreet Boys. Emojis emerged.

She'd ask, 'Isn't it 5 a.m. in Ireland now lol? How do you stay up so late?'

She asked him why she was his only Facebook friend, and why his profile photo was Garth Brooks and why he didn't post any photos at all. And he said it was because he kept his disease a secret, that he was a property developer, and he was terrified that his investors would get cold feet if they knew he was sick with a parasite. His property portfolio was situated in different time zones, so he did business at night.

Joop stole photos from the Facebook page of Dickie Herlihy the Hyundai salesman and messaged them to Skye. Dickie's six-bedroom house with the chandelier in the hallway, his ten acres of land, his pony, his speedboat. His face, his new teeth, his full head of hair.

'That's me,' he said, 'getting on in years mind.'

'Wow, you sound too good to be true,' she said, with a winking emoji. 'Surely you have a wife? Kids? What are you not telling me Vinny, winking emoji?'

And Joop said: 'Oh Skye, I had a wife, Mary, but she died a few years back. We have a son in his twenties, also called Vincent, but he's in university now studying to be a bomb disposal expert.'

'Wow,' she said. 'I bet he's as handsome as his dad lol.'

And Joop said lol back.

'Do you miss Mary? How did you guys meet?' Skye asked. 'We got pregnant out of wedlock and just got married, that's how things were back then. I do miss her. But you must move on from these painful memories or they will take over your life.' 'I'm so sorry about this Vinny. If it's not too painful to answer, how did she die?' Joop took a few minutes to respond and said, 'It's OK, Skye. She was a victim of a terror attack, a bus she was on exploded. I don't like to go over the details.' 'That is heartbreaking Vinny, you should be so proud of your son for growing up and becoming a bomb disposal expert. His momma is looking down on him with a big smile,' said Skye.

Joop then offered her money. He proposed to wire her one thousand euros to help with Aaron's next round of steroid injections. Skye took some time to respond. Joop felt the terror of abandonment and thought about killing himself. The next day, Skye declined his offer. She explained that she didn't feel comfortable accepting the money. But Joop insisted. He had just closed a huge deal in Mykonos, sold a condominium he'd developed. He was feeling very generous and wanted to help her, because he could. It would mean a lot to him if she would allow it. Skye graciously accepted. Joop took one thousand euros from the fund that was raised for him by Dickie Herlihy. It was wired via Western Union under the name Vincent Melrose.

Three days later, Skye messaged Joop a photograph of her and Aaron sharing ice cream in a booth of the restaurant she worked in.

'Big guy is killing this sundae. Thanks again, Vinny. You've really brought a smile back to his face.'

Aaron looked stronger – he looked like a normal boy of his age enjoying normal things that boys his age enjoy. A wave of pleasure and excitement jolted through Joop.

He felt like a decent and worthy person.

He felt like all the change and possibility in the world.

He felt like Bob Geldof.

He did a little barefoot line dance on the granny carpet in front of his computer monitor. He noticed the static electricity in his soles. The fizzy violence of Heineken hitting the back of the throat floated into his mind. He got a notion to buy a crate of it in Aldi. But now that he'd found love, he wasn't going to fuck it all away on drink. He couldn't stop now. If he slowed down the worm would make his head explode. He felt his hands burning as if they were fondling a small fire and experienced his first seizure. The worm was in his brain.

Skye said that Big Pharma had a cure for rat lungworm disease but they were holding it back so that they could push steroid injections. Vaccines are actually biological tracking devices created by 'you know who'. Joop agreed.

She asked him if he thought about love, if he thought about a future, and if there was another person in that future. She asked him how he could be so driven and successful in the property business despite the rat lungworm growing inside of him. Joop told Skye that he lived without any symptoms because he bathed in a Holy Well at the foot of a mountain near Thurles. A natural spring where slugs clung to the rocks. The slugs were said to worship at the feet of the hero Cúchulainn, who ate them before battle. They were blessed by the goddess Brigid and their trails sparkled with stardust from the otherworld. For thousands of years, people have travelled from all over Ireland to experience the healing power of the slugs and the water in this Holy Well.

'Of course, the doctors don't want to admit any of it,' he'd say, 'and you won't read about the well online because this is all local indigenous knowledge that was passed down orally.'

He informed Skye that he had no symptoms, no fear, no pain, no headaches, no burning of the skin. No seizures. The rat lungworm was still in him, but it was made inert by the satiating water of the Holy Well. The worm told him this in a dream. He had found the cure.

'I am living proof of the healing power of the water in the well.'

And these words that he had pulled out of his hole unfolded before Skye like a soothing blanket.

She messaged him about the photographs on Google of Thurles and the Tipperary Mountains. How it was like a fairy-tale land of grassy glens and dells and hills. She could imagine the púca and fairies emerging in the morning mist over the magical landscape. Long-haired goblins bathing under waterfalls, and white horses galloping into the sea foam and turning into diamonds. How the ancient Irish people were actually aliens who came from a star system called Zeta Reticuli. How it reminded her of the way her grandfather had described Kerry when she was a child.

And Joop said it was exactly like that.

'Maybe you and Aaron should come here and live with me? I have all this space and no one to fill it. The long hallways of my house are empty except for the sound of my own footsteps. Come here to me, Skye. Little Aaron can bathe and drink in the waters of the Holy Well. Cúchulainn's slugs can crawl all over him. He won't need any more steroid injections. He'll be free from the pain and torment, like I am. You and I will get married.'

'And what about my job, my life, my family?' asked Skye.

And Joop responded that it was fate that brought them together, and how foolish it would be to ignore the universe when it creates two souls that vibrate at the same frequency. Live fully, laugh often, love deeply.

And the voice inside of Skye, which had been sensible at one point in her life, had long been silenced by the terrible pressure and sadness and hardship of it all. She'd rather listen to hope, no matter what shape it took.

Before long, the two of them were talking about flights to Ireland. Skye still had some apprehensions. She trusted this lovely Irish man named Vinny Melrose. He had sent money after all. A faker wouldn't send money like that. But still, a niggling caution in her needed more proof. She suggested that they make video calls. Joop said that he was too old for that class of technology and it was a miracle he was even able to text her on the Facebook. Skye was endeared by this response, imagining him as a rugged man of the meadows who spoke with the mountains and the deer. Skye then intimated the possibility of video sex, hoping that this would entice him to appear on camera, and allow her to dispel any small doubts from her mind before she made one of the biggest decisions of her life.

This suggestion made Joop feel incredibly angry because Skye was pure and perfect with a sick son, and not one of these young whores that they have now, who show their tits and arseholes on the internet. He didn't say this to Skye, and instead told her that he had been looking at flights from Oahu to Shannon. That there's one in a week and that he'd wire her the money immediately.

'That's a lot of money, Vinny,' she said.

'There's no price tag on this adventure,' he said. 'Ye'll fly to Shannon. It's only a short bus to Thurles. And once ye get here, ask for the greatest line dancer to ever grace the town. You'll be shown where to find me.'

'Lol,' said Skye, 'you're hilarious Vincent. I guess that sounds like a plan. I can't believe we're actually doing this.'

The money was wired. Young Aaron was informed. Bags were packed. At Oahu Airport, Skye bought him a battery power-bank for his gaming tablet and one of those foam travel pillows to help with the pain in his neck during the long flight. She held his fingers like she'd never let them go and kissed his forehead while he slept beside her.

The warm pink sun blessed her face through the oval airplane window, and she listened to the hope in her chest. Her eyes flew out over the Pacific Ocean, across the silver cloud, and swept below the valley lakes, through the purple heather on the mountains of Thurles, the Aldi car park, slithering down the ivy that clung to the bungalow, where Joop lay firm in his acrylic recliner. The ghost of Coco's Paradise.

Himself and the rat lungworm in his brain, friend of the slugs and the rain.

Joop.

Wafting through the letter box, a warm spicy blend with a hint of freshness, complemented by top notes of mandarin and sandalwood. Heart notes of tonka bean and skatole creating a lingering seductive fragrance.

Topographia Hibernica

Giraldus de Barri attempted to defecate among a thicket of nettles on a Wexford beach. Having been constipated for several weeks, owing to his diet of hazelnuts and roasted hedgehogs. He had introduced the hedgehogs to Ireland from Wales in the previous year of 1183. The natives called them *gráinneog*, which meant 'ugly little thing'. He despised their jokes and their sideways language. The sky above Giraldus was obscured by a drinkable mist and the air stank of low tide. He hovered his buttocks over young nettles and relished the punishment of their delicate stings around his arse and thighs. He became sexually aroused. His thoughts focussed intrusively on the Ox Man of Glendalough.

Giraldus, during his travels around Ireland, had heard the tales. Shortly before the arrival of the English, a cow gave birth to a man-calf. It was the fruit of a union between a human and a cow. Giraldus began to envisage how this conception occurred. Did a savage Irish man, erect and full of animal passion, enter a female cow and impregnate her with his sperm? Or had these Irish a more sophisticated method of bovine–human copulation, akin to the invention by Daedalus of the great Minoan culture? Yes. Long before the birth of our Lord, King Minos of Crete had wished for a brilliant white bull from the sea god Poseidon. Poseidon delivered the bull on the condition that Minos would sacrifice it in his honour. But the bull was too beautiful, too powerful, too muscular, too perfect to sacrifice. King Minos kept the bull for himself in a fit of selfishness. And so, Poseidon punished Minos by enchanting his wife Pasiphaë. Pasiphaë was overcome with a deep sexual lust for the dumb animal. She ignored her husband, she became transfixed on the bull, she was hopelessly in love.

Giraldus achieved full tumescence on the Wicklow beach when he imagined Pasiphaë lying awake in the sweat of her bedstraw, pleasuring herself at the fantasy of being fucked by the white bull. He noticed the east sea breeze tickling the whiskers of his squatted hole and experienced it as the fingers of Poseidon.

Pasiphaë longed to be entwined with the bull, but could not think of how this could unfold without being crushed to death by its size. After failed attempts at arousing the bull, she came to accept that the creature wasn't attracted to her. This bull did not want a human the way Pasiphaë wanted the bull. Her heart was breaking, but she was determined to mate and so decided to become a cow. She approached the inventor Daedalus and demanded that he construct a beautiful wooden cow costume in which she would conceal her human body. A cow so alluring that the bull would be seduced. Daedalus obliged and Pasiphaë fulfilled her wish of fornicating with the beast.

Giraldus, at this point, was giddy with these images in his mind, and commenced masturbating in the thicket of nettles on the Wicklow beach. He moaned like a corncrake. The Norman men-at-arms who were guarding Giraldus did not take notice; they assumed he was just having another difficult shit in the nettles.

Giraldus imagined Pasiphaë curled up in the false cow with the skin of her arse poking out the back. He saw the rotund white bull mount the contraption on hind legs and ravish Pasiphaë, steam puffing from its nostrils and condensing in drips on the wooden hide. He heard the song of her muffled orgasms in his brain. His mind's eye in the bull's forehead. Giraldus was the bull now and he pummelled the skin and timber of the womancow. Pasiphaë became pregnant from the union and bore offspring in the form of the Minotaur, the terrible creature with a man's chiselled body and the head of a bull, who ate children and was confined to a labyrinth on Crete.

But as Giraldus navigated the vinegar strokes of climax, he squandered his erection with unwelcome reflections on the Ox Man of Glendalough. This big stupid Godhelpus of a thing. Fully human except for possessing a cow's hooves instead of hands and feet, the fruit of a randy Irish man and a common field cow. Pale, sweaty and dung-thighed in a ditch. The Ox Man of Glendalough was born with flapping skin. He wasn't fearsome like the Minotaur, or worthy of being woven in myth or carved into a statue. Pagan priests visited the Ox Man with offerings of novelty-sized Communion wafers and he would defile the flesh of the Lord with his clumsy, ruminant hooves. The natives found this funny. Yes, man in form, but ox in extremity: hooves for hands, hooves for feet, joints connecting, disjoining. Baldness, a deformity, crowned his head. No great horns or snout, hairless before and behind, save for down in scattered patches. Eyes, large, round, oxen in hue, stared from a face flat to the mouth, noseless but for two orifices, breathing, snorting. Speechless, his utterances were but the lowing of a cow. It was put to death in the court of Maurice to end the misery of its existence, and not one Irish witness could decide if they should call it murder or venery.

Giraldus was angry and flaccid now, his wank destroyed by the Ox Man of Glendalough. Why do these damned Irish have to do everything backwards, he thought? Why must everything be a joke to them? Had they been contacted by the great Minoan culture at some point in their wretched history? Had they been gifted the ideas of the Greeks and, instead of civilising themselves, turned the myths on their heads for japes? The marbled musculature of the Minotaur, the erotic passion of Pasiphaë, the ingenuity of Daedalus's sex cow reduced to a beige blob full of hooves? Why would they do this? They have done to the Minotaur what they have done to the Gospel of Christ.

Giraldus abandoned the wank and returned to other matters. He puckered his hoop. No interior matter would expunge. Too much hedgehog slowed his bowels. He experienced shame for fantasising about the desires of Pasiphaë and again stung his grundle with nettles as contrition before God. He begged for succour from St Augustine. He pushed until a wormy vein presented on the side of his forehead, and he meditated on Leviticus: 'And if a woman approach unto any beast, and lie down thereto, thou shalt kill the woman, and the beast: they shall surely be put to death; their blood shall be upon them.'

Near by and extremely vigilant, the men-at-arms listened without comment as Giraldus began to argue loudly with his own rectum. He stared down betwixt his haunches and conversed with his rectum as if he were scolding a hound.

He grew furious with Roderic, the King of Connaught, who possessed a domesticated white goat, distinguished by its silken hair and the extent of its horns. This goat had engaged in a beastly manner with the woman to whom it had been entrusted, it having been lured to serve as the means of satisfying her unnatural desires. 'O heinous and shameful act!' howled Giraldus. 'How savagely does the master of beasts, forsaking her natural prerogatives, stoop to the level of heathen, when she, a being endowed with reason, consents to such union with a brute!'

His anus did not respond.

Giraldus was pure fuming with Duvenald, King of Limerick, who had a woman with a beard extending to her navel, and, furthermore, a crest resembling that of a yearling colt that spanned from the summit of her neck to her backbone and was enveloped in hair. 'This woman, distinguished by two extraordinary deformities, was not a hermaphrodite. Do you hear? But, in other aspects, she possessed the attributes of a woman. And she was a continual presence at the court, a subject of both mockery and astonishment. The chimera was not defined as either male or female or animal. And, in the cultivation of a lengthy beard, she adhered to the customs of her land. Duvenald, the savage king, lay with the horse woman of Limerick in his marital bed each night before God.'

His anus did not respond.

And Giraldus refused to acknowledge the titles of the leaders of the land. He steadied his breathing, slow from the diaphragm, as if he were in labour and said, 'There exist matters which modesty might forbid me to recount. A sordid tale may cast a shadow upon its teller, but it may also reveal his art. Cover your ears, men, for in the distant northern reaches of Ulster, at Kenel Cunil, resides a people who practise a most abominable rite in creating their king. Assembled in one place, a white mare is brought to them, and the one to be crowned, not as a noble but as a beast, not as a monarch but as an outlaw, comes before the people on all fours. He then partakes in bestial intercourse with the horse and professes himself to also be a beast at the precise moment of ejaculation. The mare is dispatched with an axe, cut in pieces, and boiled; a bath from the broth is prepared for the man. Sitting in this, he eats of the flesh, which is brought to him, the people standing round partaking of it too. He is also required to drink of the broth in which he is bathed, not drawing it in any vessel, nor even in his hands, but lapping it with his mouth like a duck. These unrighteous rites, being duly accomplished, is how these animals crown their kings on this island of Ireland, the Kingdom of Beasts. Expunge, expunge yourself my rueful hole, or away to Purgatory with you,' Gerald proclaimed to his sphincter.

The men-at-arms struggled to conceal their smirks upon hearing Giraldus condemn his own rectum to the abyss. Giraldus then discerned the promise of a movement in his gut and shifted focus to the plain people of the land. Slightly calmer and sensing impending relief, his words grew more forgiving.

'The sole endeavour to which I observe this people dedicating a commendable diligence is their performance upon musical instruments. In this art, they are unsurpassed in skill by any other nation I have ever witnessed. Yet, though they are generously blessed with nature's bounty, their want of civilization, manifest in both their attire and intellectual cultivation, renders them a people savage and animal. Immersed in sloth, their greatest delight is to be exempt from toil, their richest possession is the enjoyment of liberty. The Irish are a rude race, subsisting on the produce of their cattle only, and living themselves like beasts. They are cows, still adhering to the customs of the pasture. This nation, holding agricultural labour in contempt, scarcely valuing the wealth of towns, are exceedingly averse to civil institution. They lead the same life their fathers did in the woods. The forests of Ireland also abound with fir trees, producing frankincense and incense. There are even veins of metals in the bowels of the earth, which, from the same idle disposition, are not extracted for wealth. They are a nation prone to treachery. Their deceit is most alert when they think you are off guard, and they'll seize that moment to betray you, using their cunning to catch you unawares.'

His anus replied with an involuntary wink of the fundament and commenced the mechanics of evacuation. 'Expunge, expunge, expunge, damn you,' Giraldus said to his own arse. Immersed in its silent soliloquy, a moment as fleeting as the Wicklow winds, as from him descended a dark, firm relic, settling into the sands of Éireann, stories entwined. Rabbit-formed. A pebble of dung, wretched in its ambition.

He sighed out a temporary relief. Walking away from his efforts, he enunciated to the men, 'The judgement of God sent me to teach the Irish a lesson. The real evil with which we will have to contend is the moral evil of the selfish, perverse, and turbulent character of the people.'

Giraldus huddled himself in among the protection of the men-at-arms as they moved along the beach. The sails of their ship poked over a mound, moored in the distance. They would return to England with their tales between their heads. The most senior soldier said, 'Forgive me Archdeacon, but it wasn't wise to take that long in the open, the natives could have struck then. They hide in this mist.' 'It was worth it,' said Giraldus, 'that was a brilliant shit.'